Simone:
The Best Monster Ever!

Text and illustrations © 2017 Rémy Simard
Translation © 2017 Owlkids Books

Published in English in 2017 by Owlkids Books Inc.

Originally published in Quebec under the title *Simone, joli monstre!* in 2016 by Bayard Canada Livres.
This book contains comics that were previously published in various issues of the magazine *J'Aime Lire*.
The comics on pages 12, 23, 34, 38, 39, and 41 are previously unpublished.

Published in Canada by
Owlkids Books Inc.
10 Lower Spadina Avenue
Toronto, ON M5V 2Z2

Published in the United States by
Owlkids Books Inc.
1700 Fourth Street
Berkeley, CA 94710

Owlkids Books acknowledges the financial support of the Canada Council for the Arts, the
Ontario Arts Council, the Government of Canada through the Canada Book Fund (CBF)
and the Government of Ontario through the Ontario Media Development Corporation's
Book Initiative for our publishing activities.

Library and Archives Canada Cataloguing in Publication

Simard, Rémy
[Simone, jolie monstre. English]
    Simone : the best monster ever! / written and illustrated
by Rémy Simard.

Translation of: Simone, jolie monstre!
ISBN 978-1-77147-293-7 (hardback)

    I. Graphic novels. I. Title. II. Title: Simone, jolie monstre.
English

PN6734.S55S55 2016   j741.5'971   C2016-906101-9

Library of Congress Control Number: 2016956083

Translated by: Karen Li
English Version edited by: Jennifer MacKinnon
English Version designed by: Danielle Arbour

ONTARIO ARTS COUNCIL
CONSEIL DES ARTS DE L'ONTARIO
an Ontario government agency
un organisme du gouvernement de l'Ontario

Canada Council   Conseil des Arts
for the Arts   du Canada

Canadä

Manufactured in Sonepat, Haryana, India, in November 2016, by Replika Press Pvt. Ltd
Job #BYPC-4/11373

A   B   C   D   E   F

Publisher of Chirp, chickaDEE and OWL
www.owlkidsbooks.com | Owlkids Books is a division of   Bayard
CANADA

Simone: The Best Monster Ever!

Written and illustrated by
Rémy Simard

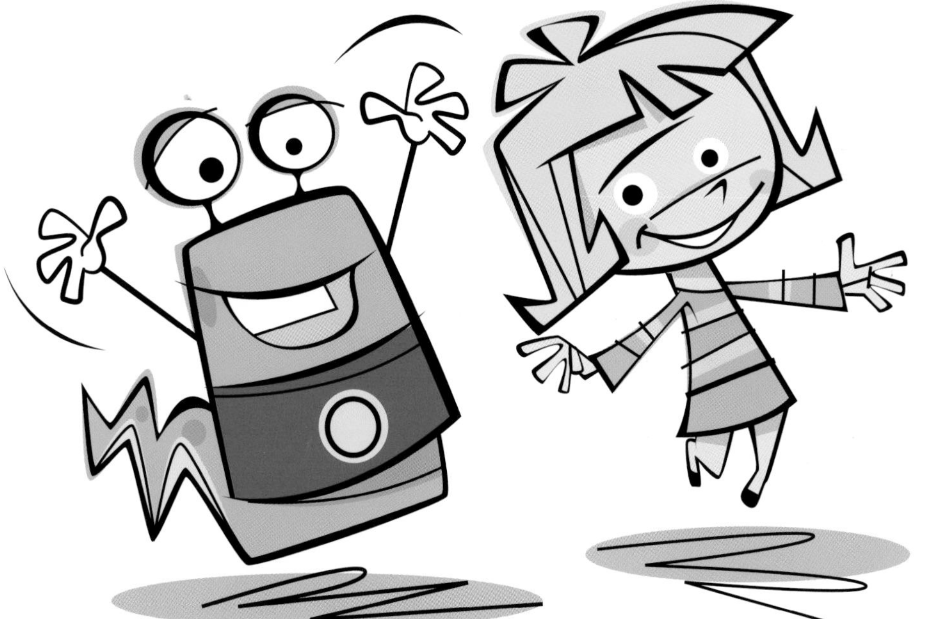

Owlkids Books

The Monster in My Closet

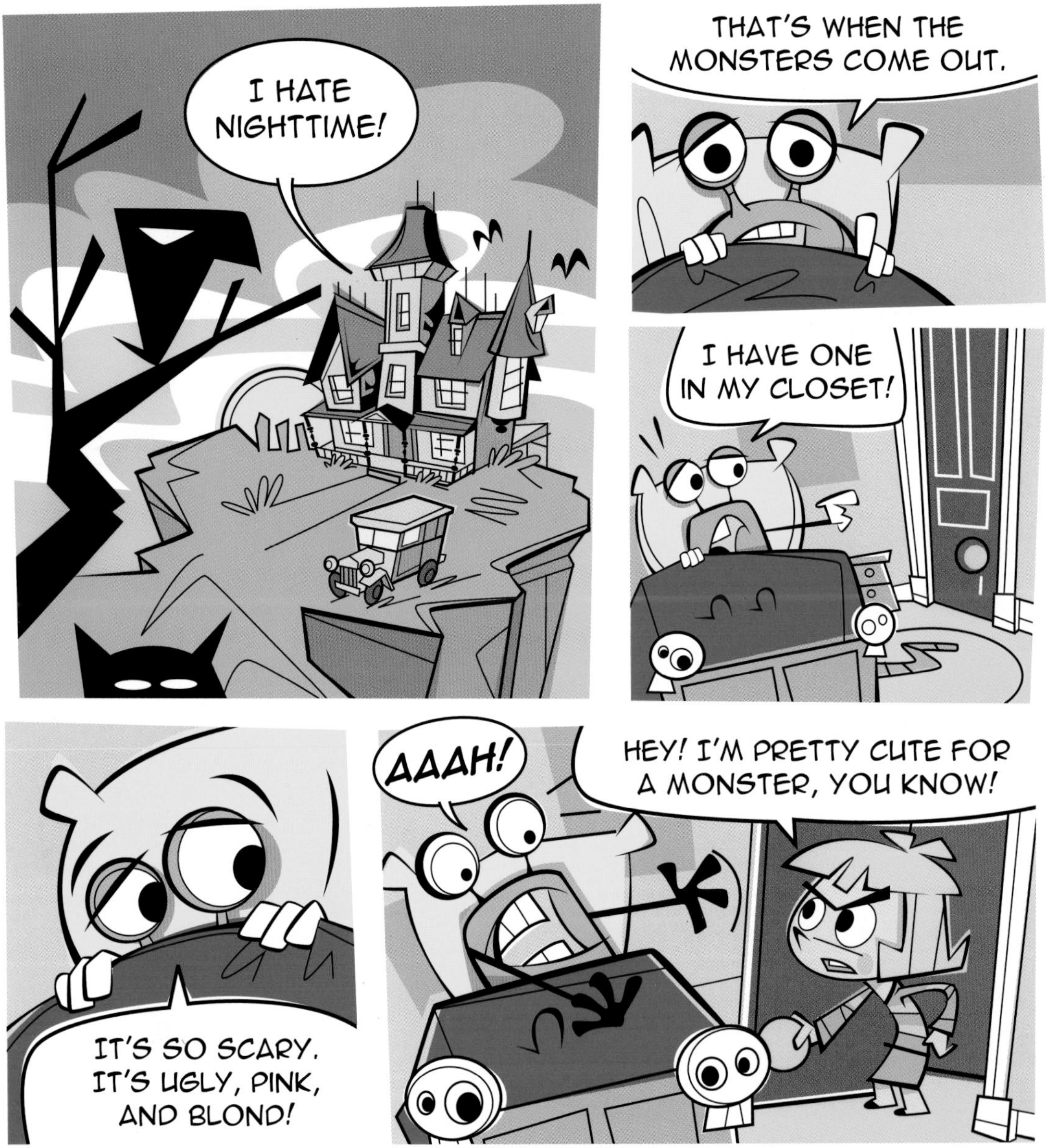
I HATE NIGHTTIME!
THAT'S WHEN THE MONSTERS COME OUT.
I HAVE ONE IN MY CLOSET!
IT'S SO SCARY. IT'S UGLY, PINK, AND BLOND!
AAAH!
HEY! I'M PRETTY CUTE FOR A MONSTER, YOU KNOW!

Halloween...Every Day!

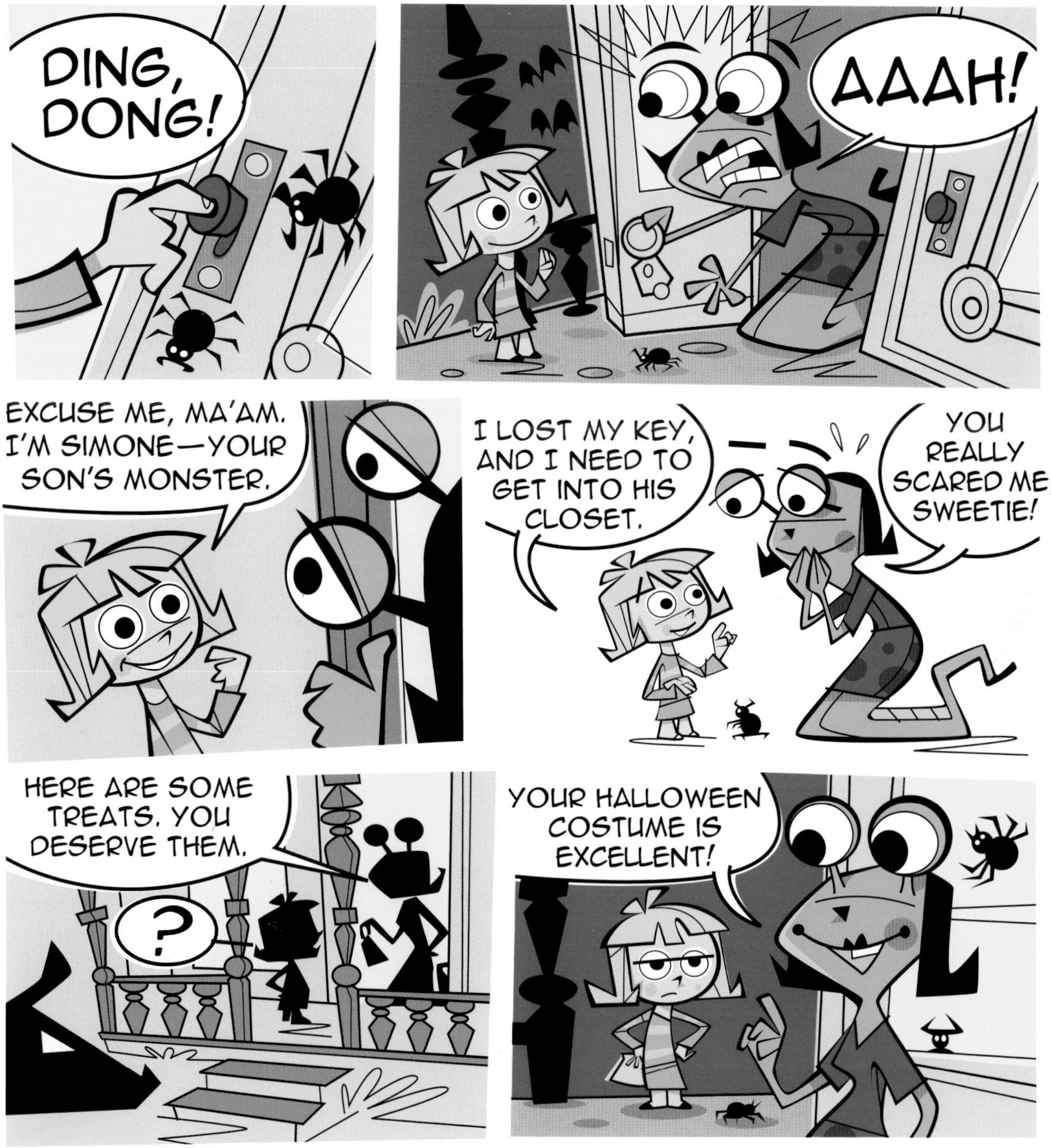
DING, DONG!
AAAH!
EXCUSE ME, MA'AM. I'M SIMONE—YOUR SON'S MONSTER.
I LOST MY KEY, AND I NEED TO GET INTO HIS CLOSET.
YOU REALLY SCARED ME, SWEETIE!
HERE ARE SOME TREATS. YOU DESERVE THEM.
?
YOUR HALLOWEEN COSTUME IS EXCELLENT!

A Side of Broccoli?

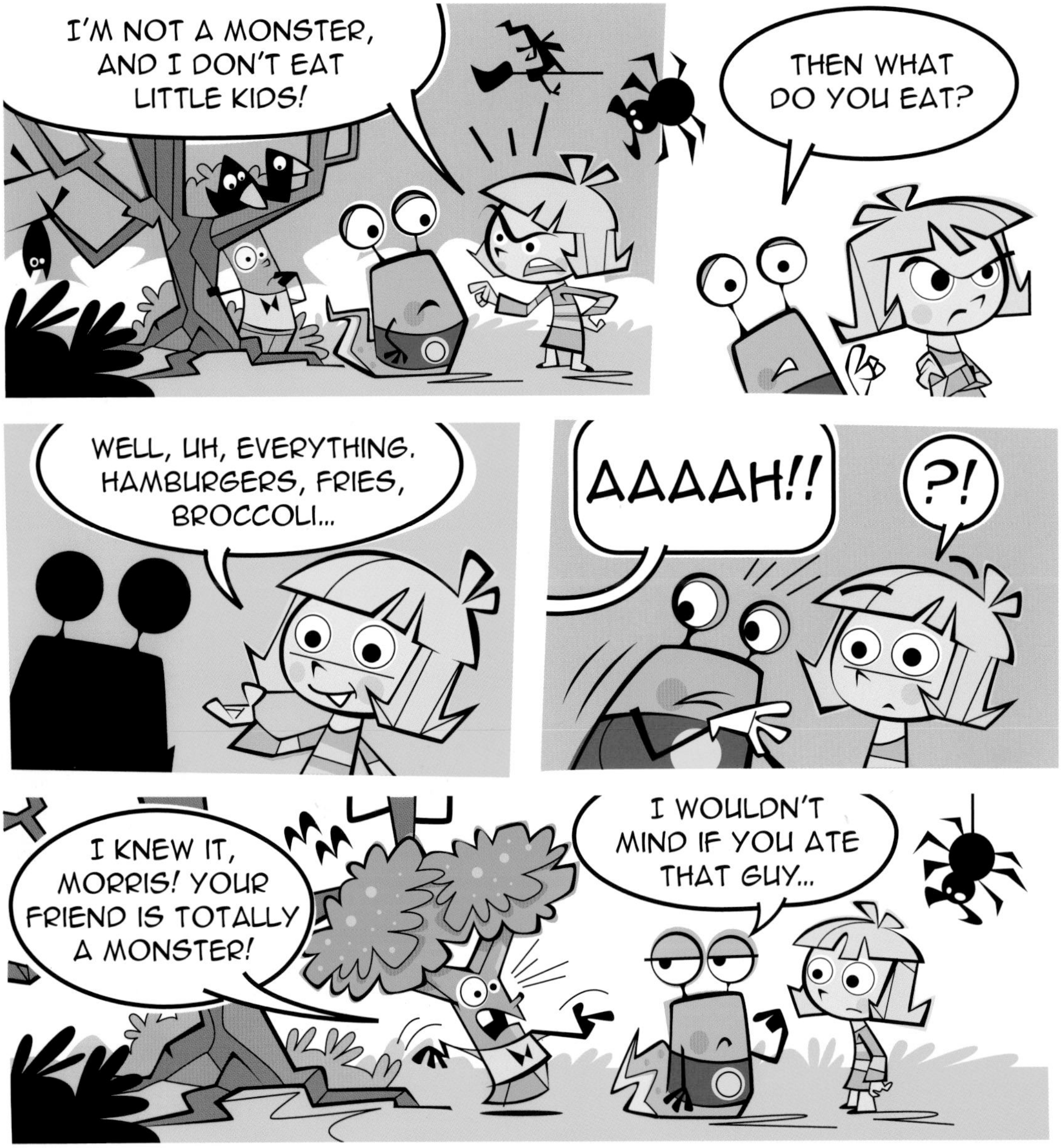

I'M NOT A MONSTER, AND I DON'T EAT LITTLE KIDS!
THEN WHAT DO YOU EAT?
WELL, UH, EVERYTHING. HAMBURGERS, FRIES, BROCCOLI...
AAAAH!!
?!
I KNEW IT, MORRIS! YOUR FRIEND IS TOTALLY A MONSTER!
I WOULDN'T MIND IF YOU ATE THAT GUY...

Santa Simone

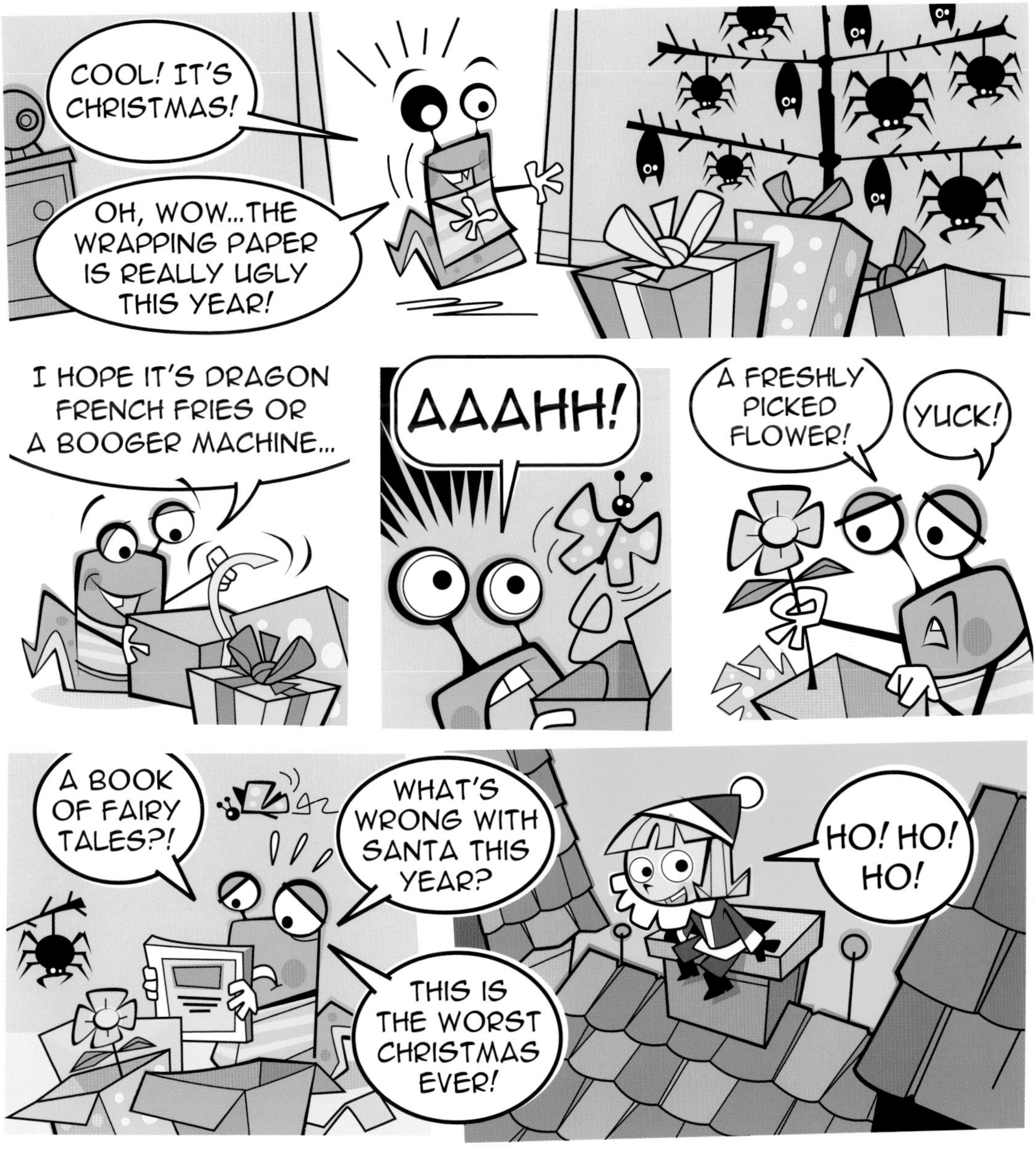

COOL! IT'S CHRISTMAS!
OH, WOW...THE WRAPPING PAPER IS REALLY UGLY THIS YEAR!
I HOPE IT'S DRAGON FRENCH FRIES OR A BOOGER MACHINE...
AAAHH!
A FRESHLY PICKED FLOWER!
YUCK!
A BOOK OF FAIRY TALES?!
WHAT'S WRONG WITH SANTA THIS YEAR?
THIS IS THE WORST CHRISTMAS EVER!
HO! HO! HO!

WARNING! Hug Alert!

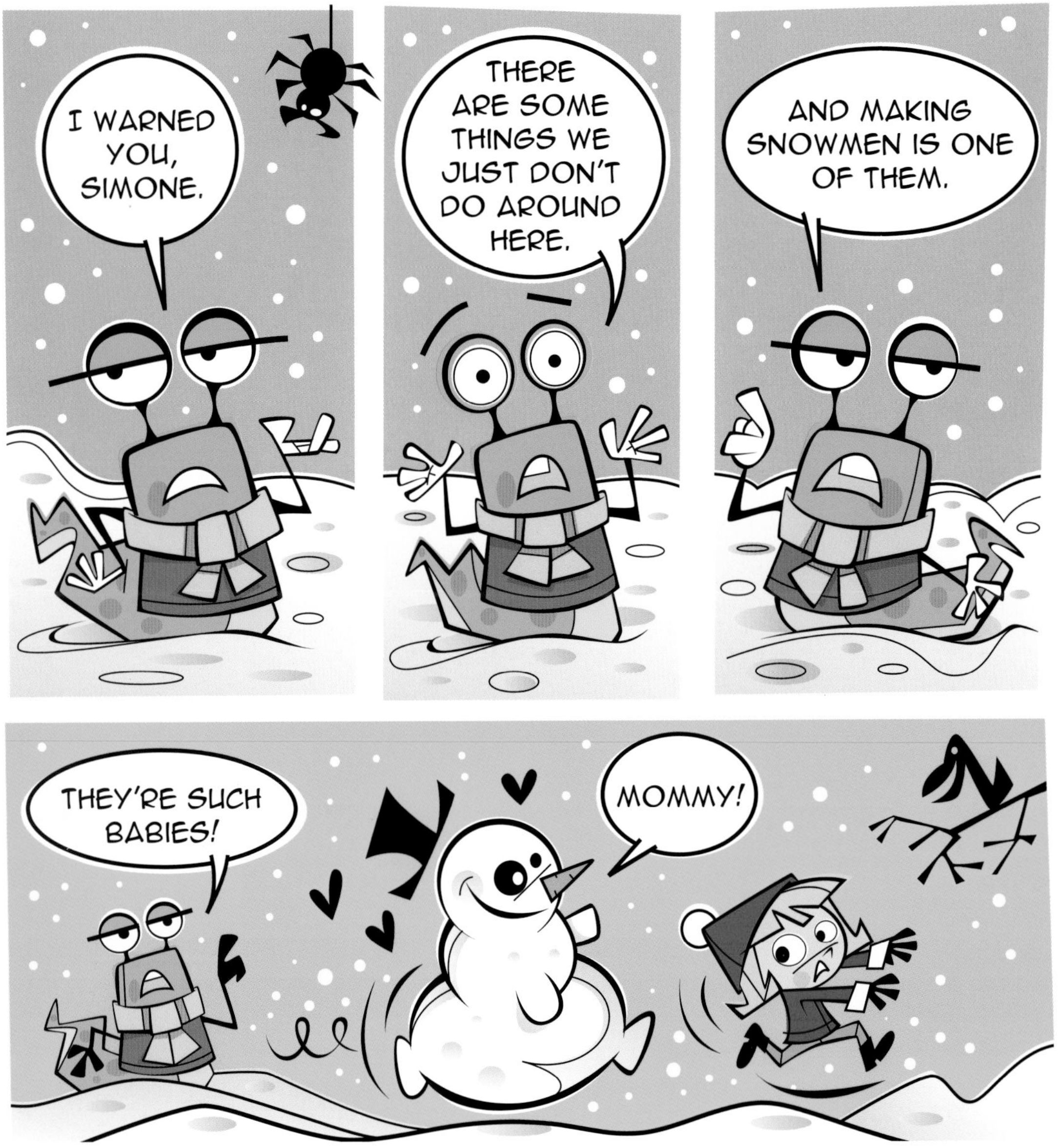

I WARNED YOU, SIMONE.
THERE ARE SOME THINGS WE JUST DON'T DO AROUND HERE.
AND MAKING SNOWMEN IS ONE OF THEM.
THEY'RE SUCH BABIES!
MOMMY!

Dreaming in Color

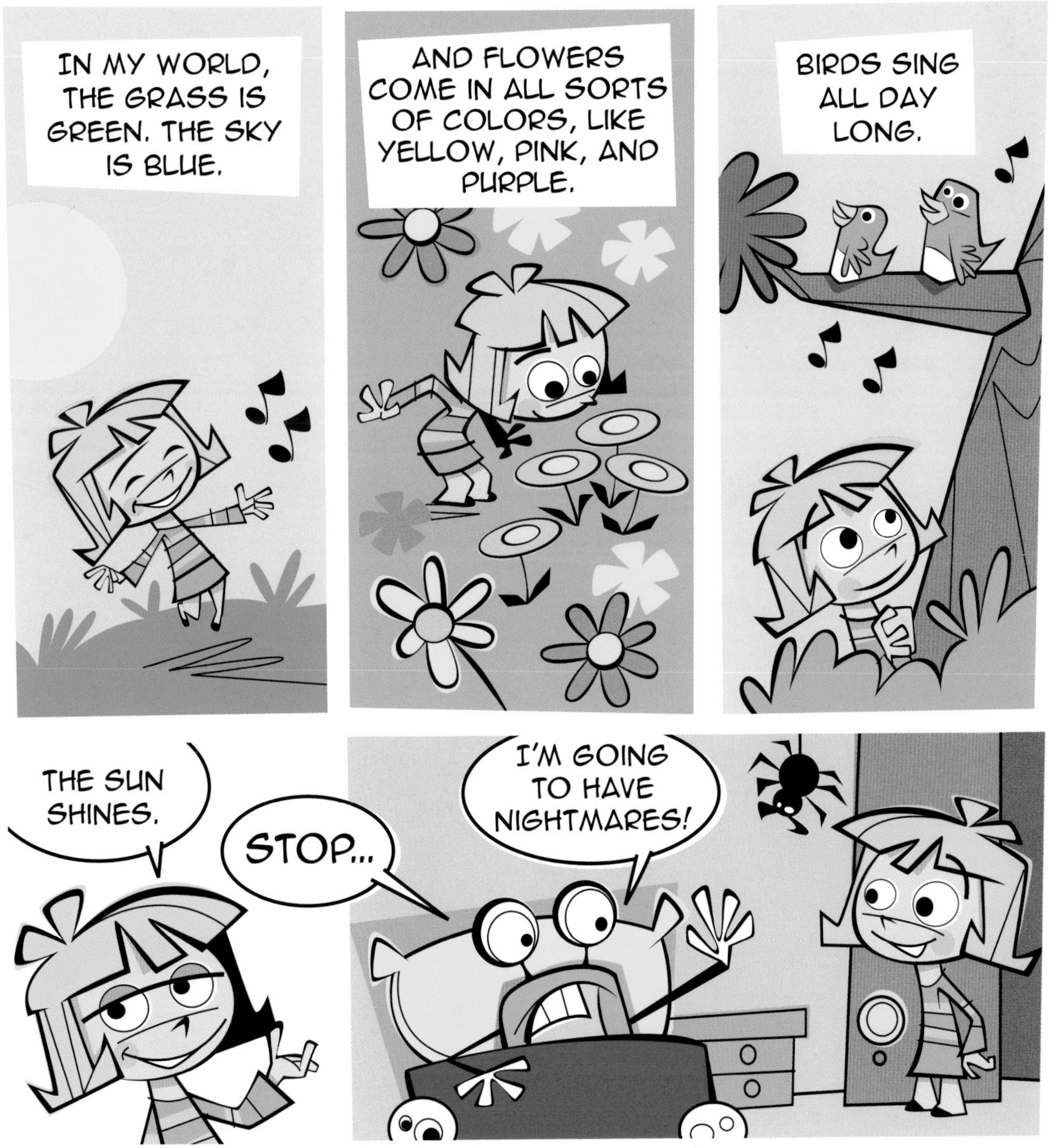

IN MY WORLD, THE GRASS IS GREEN. THE SKY IS BLUE.
AND FLOWERS COME IN ALL SORTS OF COLORS, LIKE YELLOW, PINK, AND PURPLE.
BIRDS SING ALL DAY LONG.
THE SUN SHINES.
STOP...
I'M GOING TO HAVE NIGHTMARES!

Buried Treasure

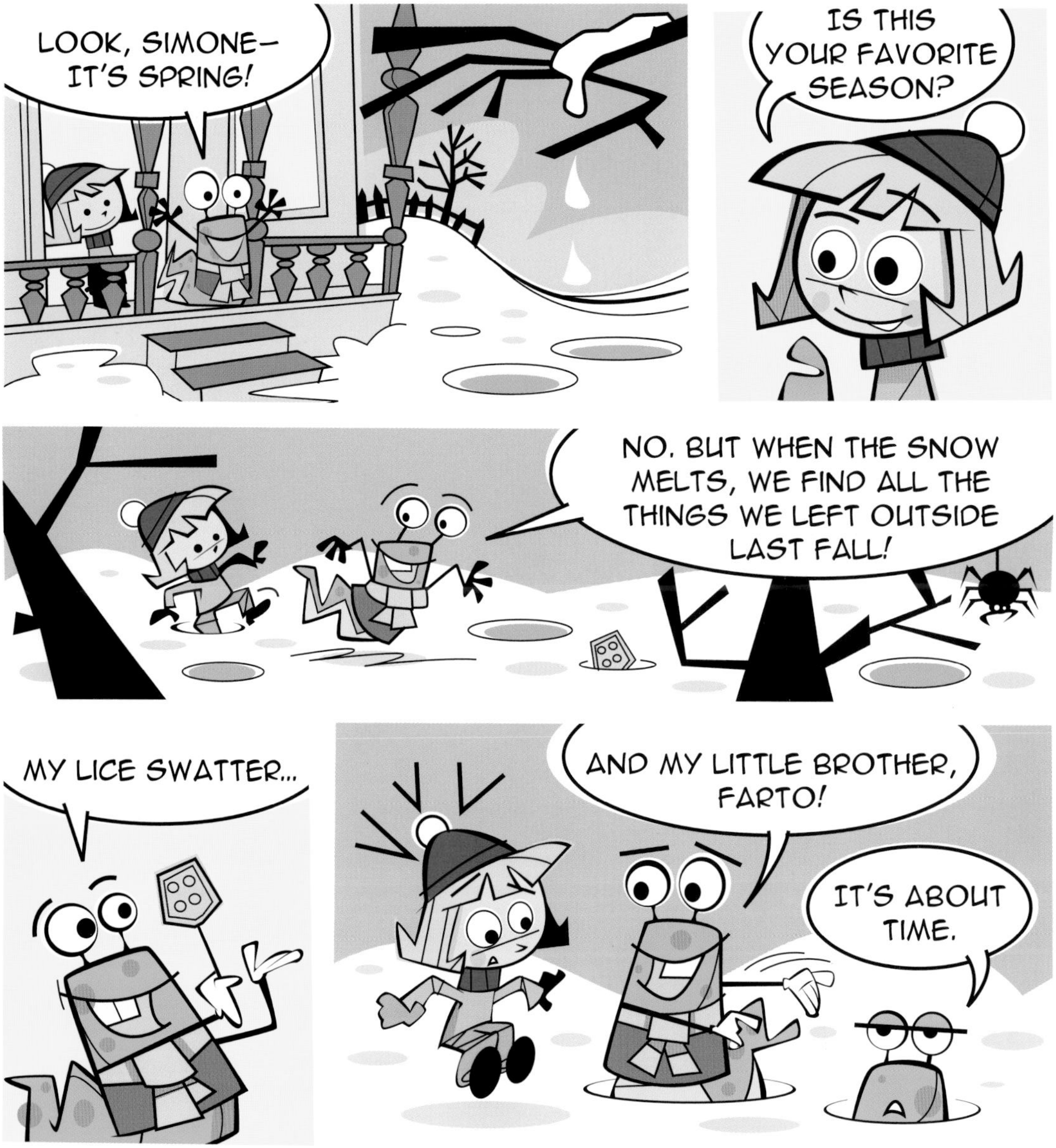

LOOK, SIMONE— IT'S SPRING!
IS THIS YOUR FAVORITE SEASON?
NO. BUT WHEN THE SNOW MELTS, WE FIND ALL THE THINGS WE LEFT OUTSIDE LAST FALL!
MY LICE SWATTER...
AND MY LITTLE BROTHER, FARTO!
IT'S ABOUT TIME.

Too Cute!

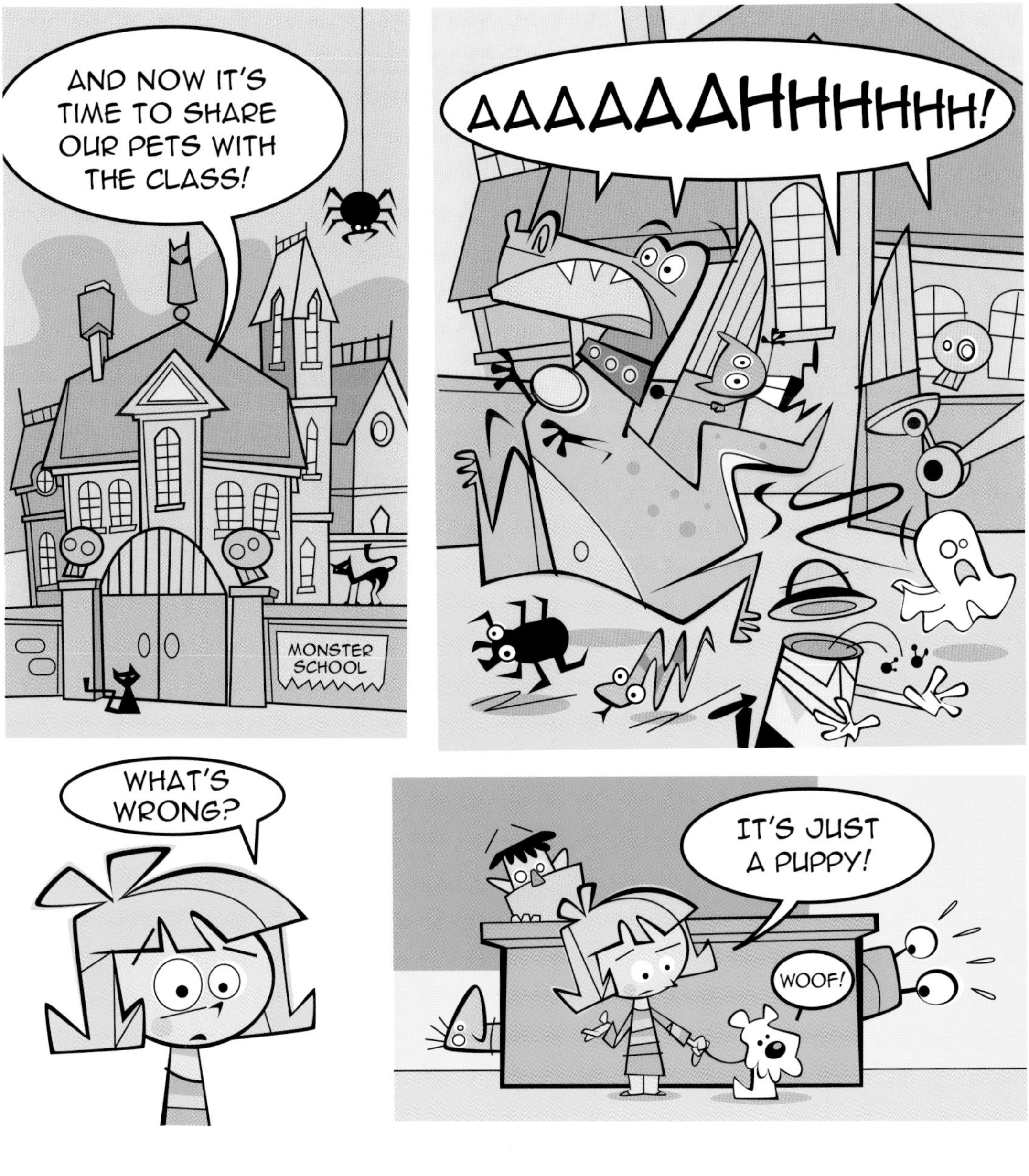
AND NOW IT'S TIME TO SHARE OUR PETS WITH THE CLASS!
MONSTER SCHOOL
AAAAAAHHHHHH!
WHAT'S WRONG?
IT'S JUST A PUPPY!
WOOF!

A Wild Ride

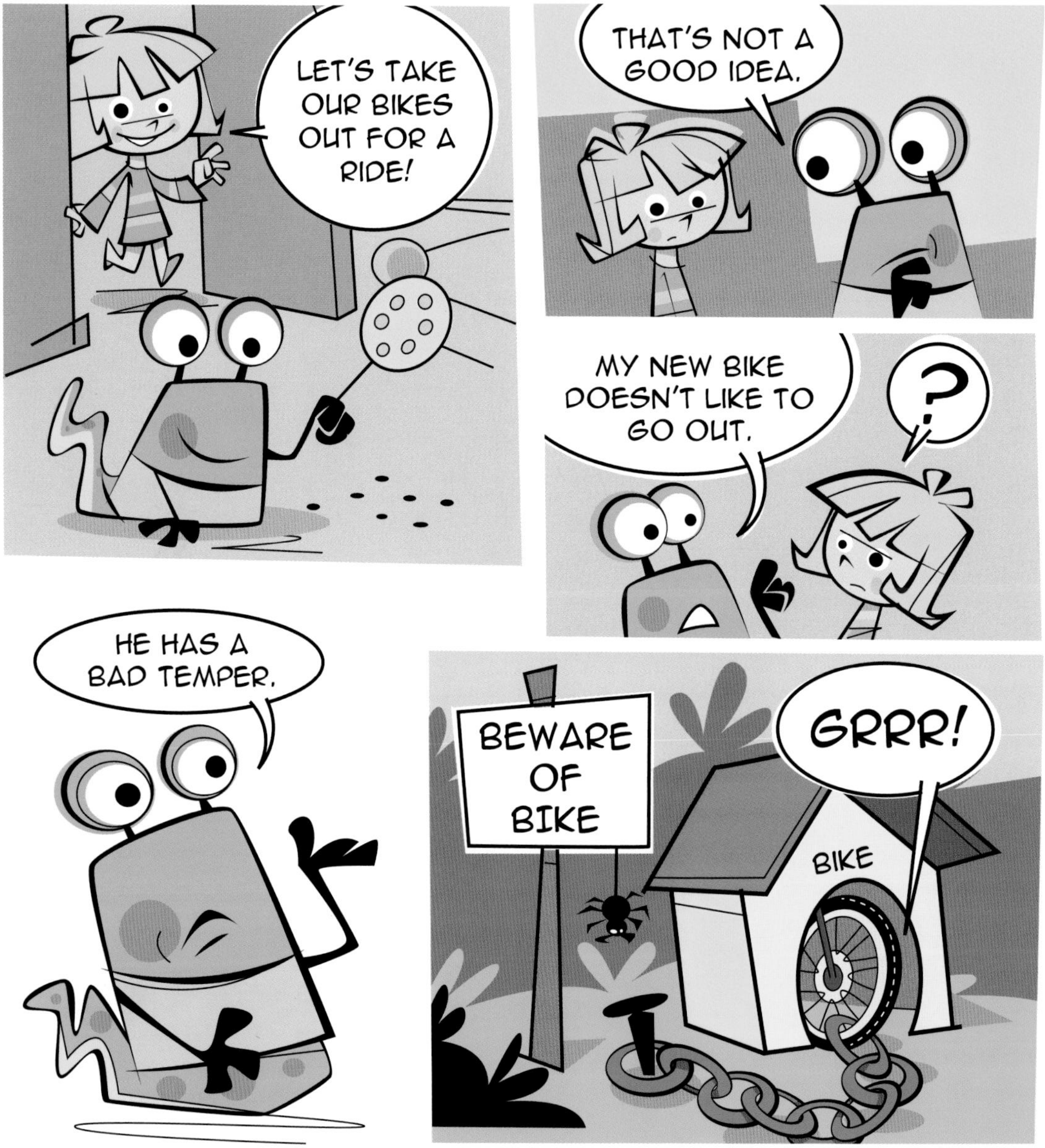

LET'S TAKE OUR BIKES OUT FOR A RIDE!
THAT'S NOT A GOOD IDEA.
MY NEW BIKE DOESN'T LIKE TO GO OUT.
?
HE HAS A BAD TEMPER.
BEWARE OF BIKE
GRRR!
BIKE

Happy Birthday!

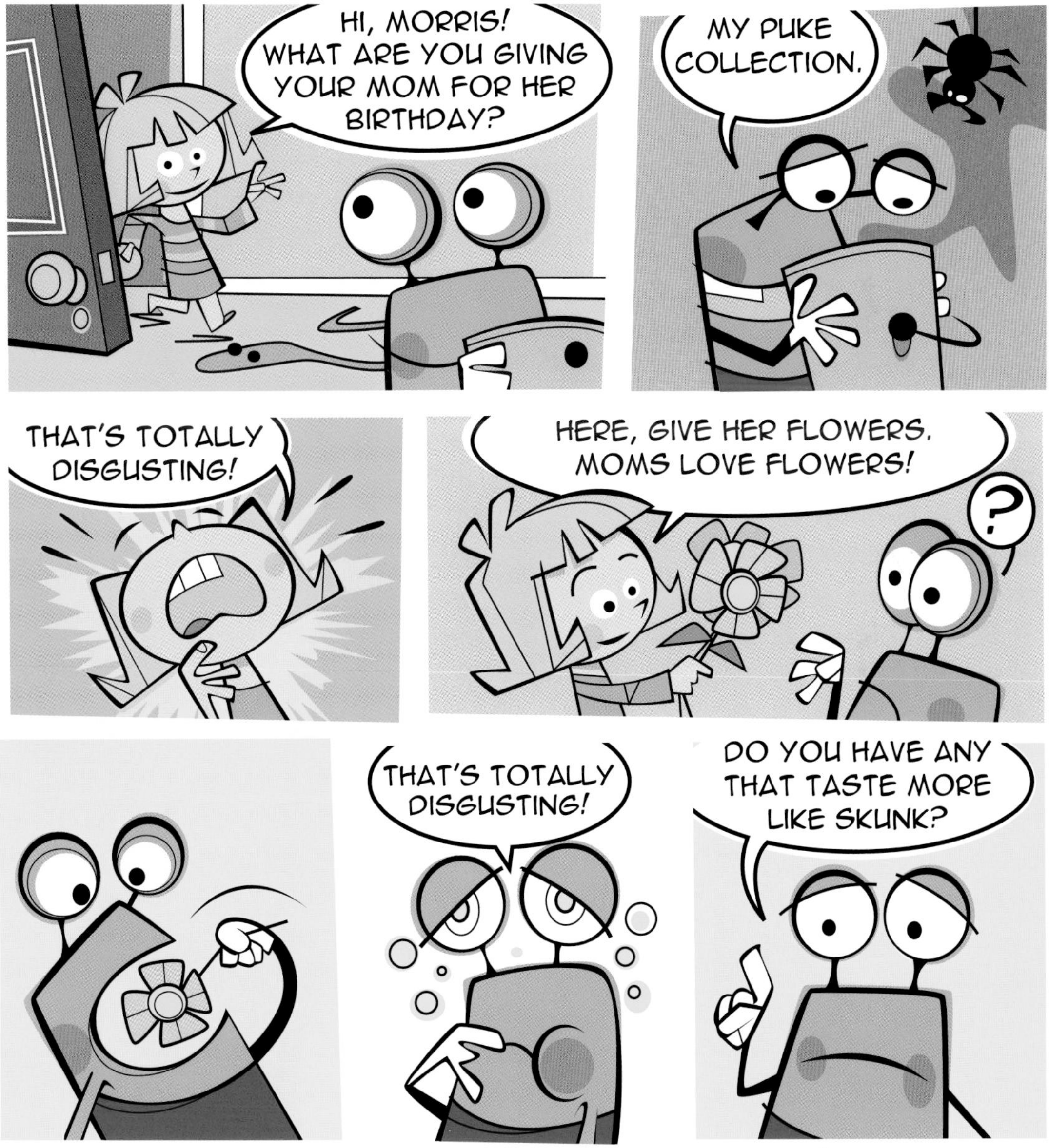
HI, MORRIS! WHAT ARE YOU GIVING YOUR MOM FOR HER BIRTHDAY?
MY PUKE COLLECTION.
THAT'S TOTALLY DISGUSTING!
HERE, GIVE HER FLOWERS. MOMS LOVE FLOWERS!
?
THAT'S TOTALLY DISGUSTING!
DO YOU HAVE ANY THAT TASTE MORE LIKE SKUNK?

Good Behavior

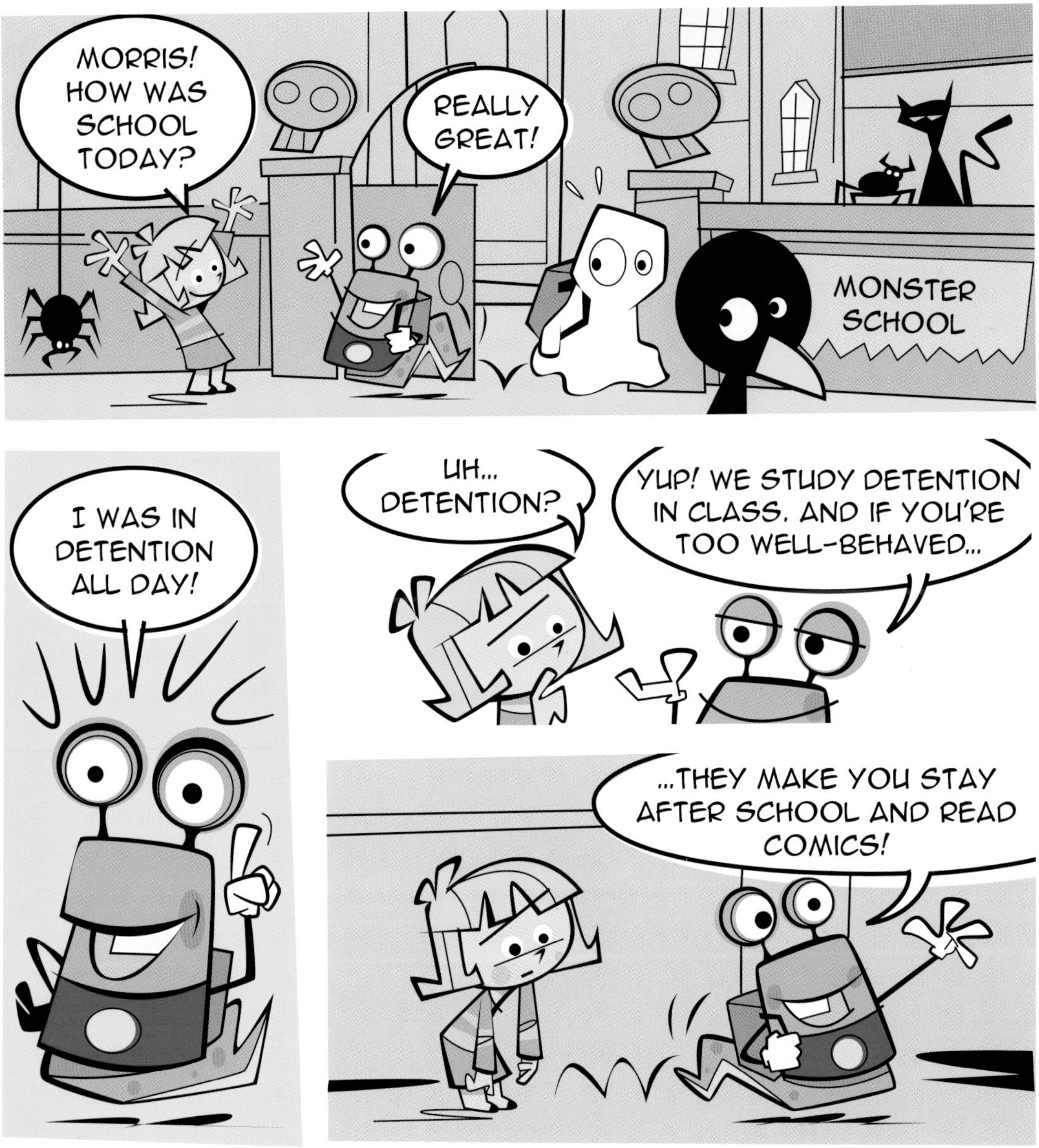
MORRIS! HOW WAS SCHOOL TODAY?
REALLY GREAT!
MONSTER SCHOOL
I WAS IN DETENTION ALL DAY!
UH... DETENTION?
YUP! WE STUDY DETENTION IN CLASS. AND IF YOU'RE TOO WELL-BEHAVED...
...THEY MAKE YOU STAY AFTER SCHOOL AND READ COMICS!

Dropping the Ball

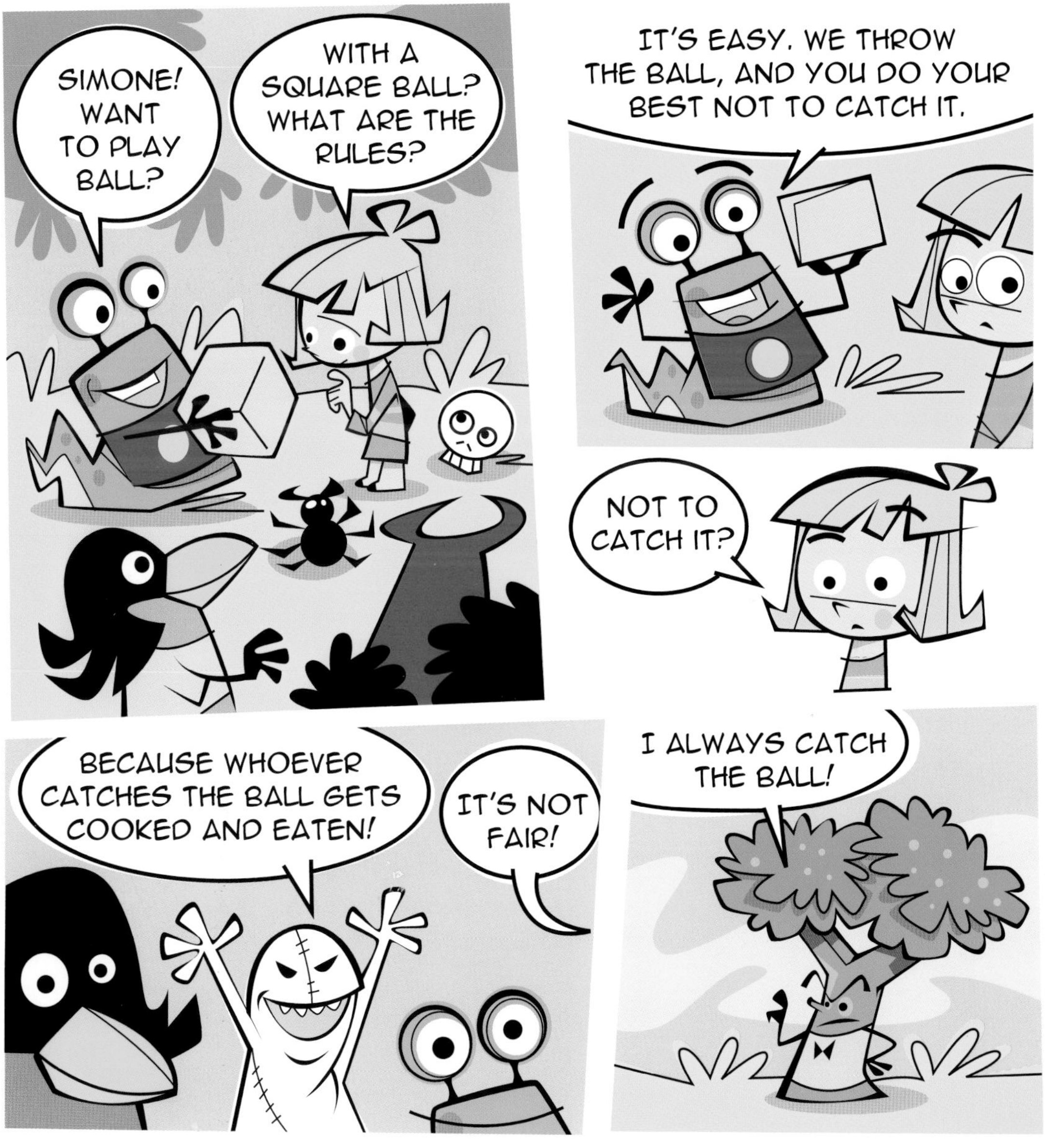

SIMONE! WANT TO PLAY BALL?
WITH A SQUARE BALL? WHAT ARE THE RULES?
IT'S EASY. WE THROW THE BALL, AND YOU DO YOUR BEST NOT TO CATCH IT.
NOT TO CATCH IT?
BECAUSE WHOEVER CATCHES THE BALL GETS COOKED AND EATEN!
IT'S NOT FAIR!
I ALWAYS CATCH THE BALL!

Super Scary Simone!

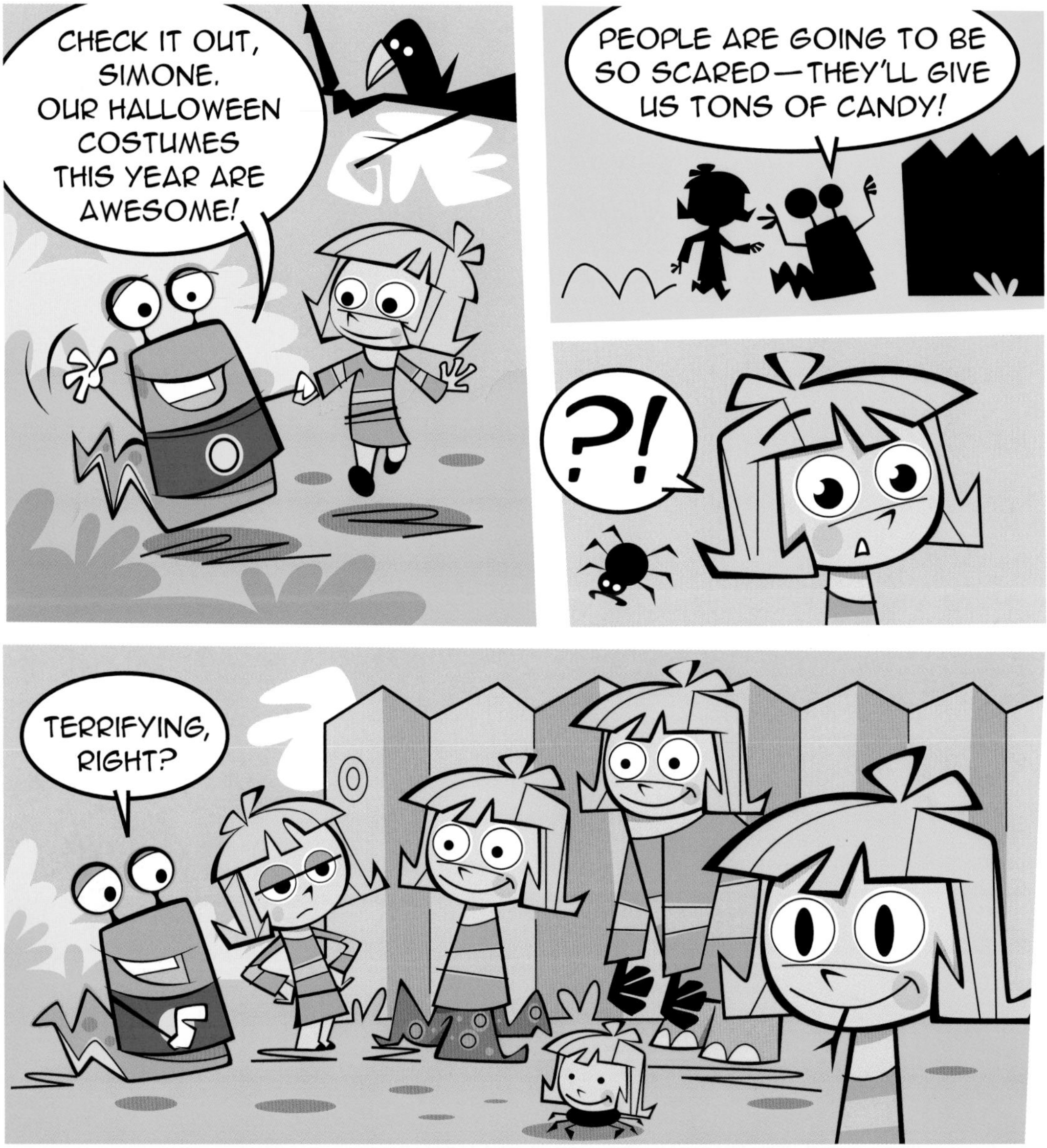

CHECK IT OUT, SIMONE. OUR HALLOWEEN COSTUMES THIS YEAR ARE AWESOME!
PEOPLE ARE GOING TO BE SO SCARED—THEY'LL GIVE US TONS OF CANDY!
?!
TERRIFYING, RIGHT?

A Monstrous Request

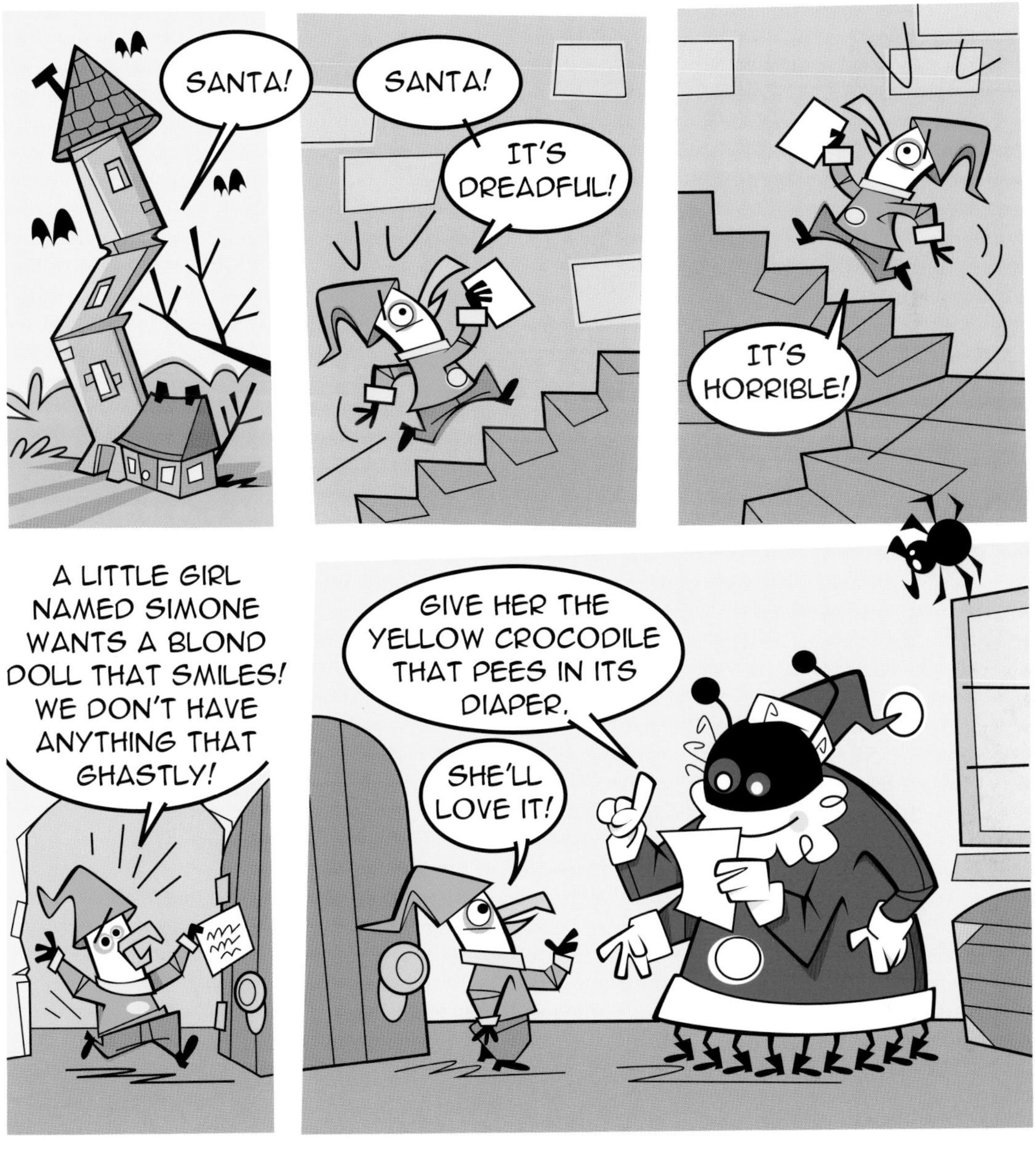
SANTA!
SANTA!
IT'S DREADFUL!
IT'S HORRIBLE!
A LITTLE GIRL NAMED SIMONE WANTS A BLOND DOLL THAT SMILES! WE DON'T HAVE ANYTHING THAT GHASTLY!
GIVE HER THE YELLOW CROCODILE THAT PEES IN ITS DIAPER.
SHE'LL LOVE IT!

Terrible New Year

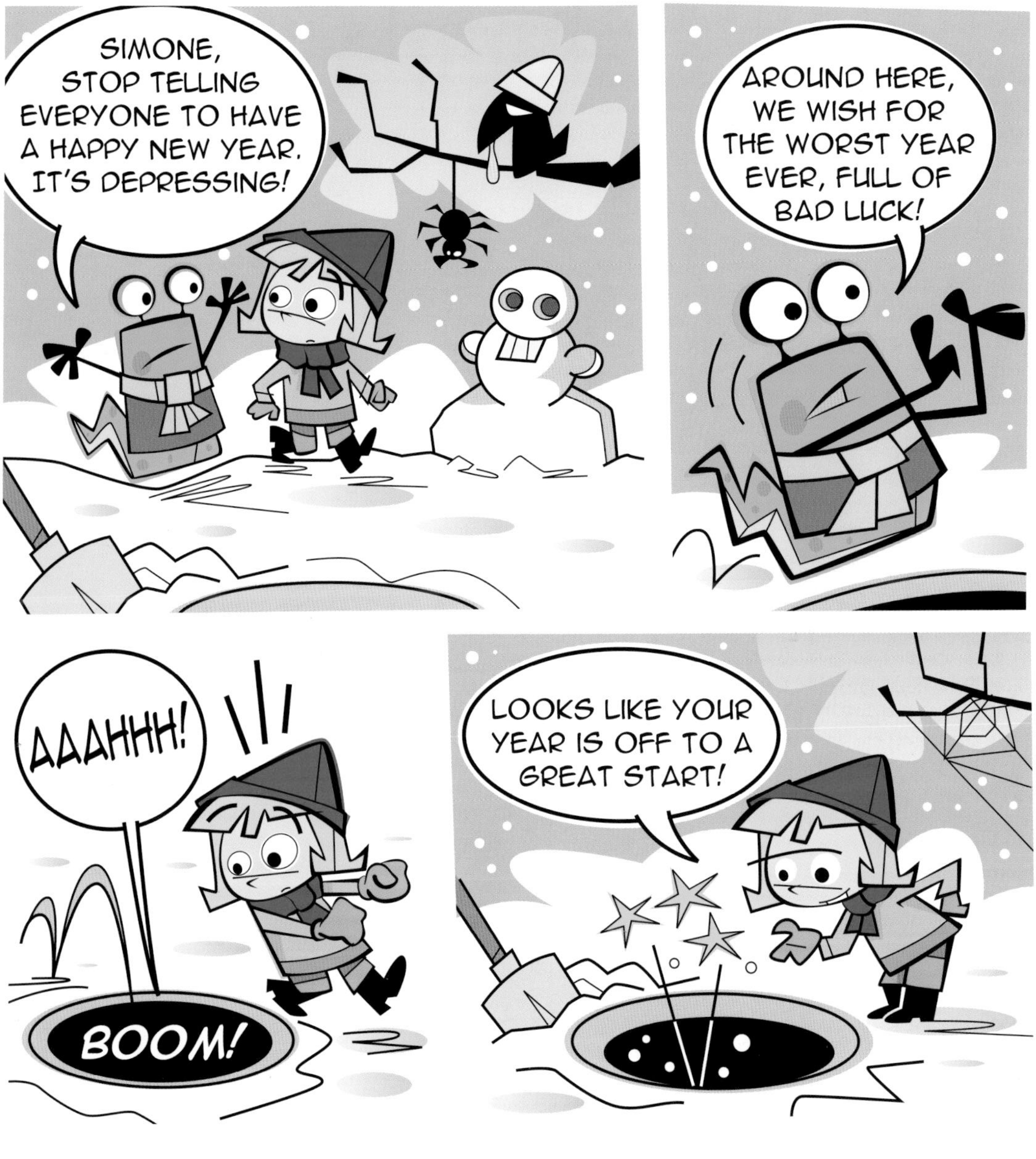
SIMONE, STOP TELLING EVERYONE TO HAVE A HAPPY NEW YEAR. IT'S DEPRESSING!
AROUND HERE, WE WISH FOR THE WORST YEAR EVER, FULL OF BAD LUCK!
AAAHHH!
BOOM!
LOOKS LIKE YOUR YEAR IS OFF TO A GREAT START!

Chocolate!

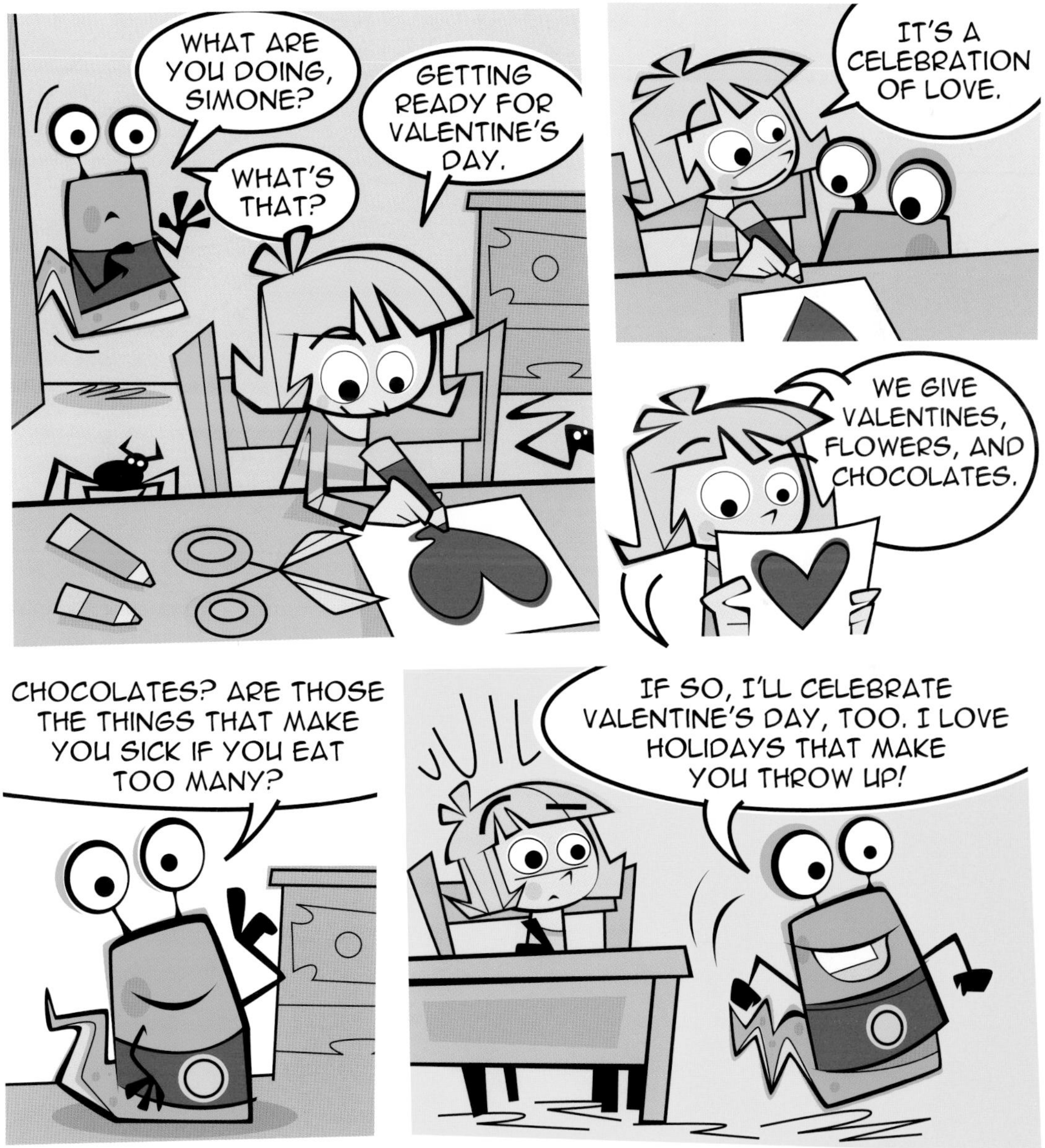
WHAT ARE YOU DOING, SIMONE?
GETTING READY FOR VALENTINE'S DAY.
WHAT'S THAT?
IT'S A CELEBRATION OF LOVE.
WE GIVE VALENTINES, FLOWERS, AND CHOCOLATES.
CHOCOLATES? ARE THOSE THE THINGS THAT MAKE YOU SICK IF YOU EAT TOO MANY?
IF SO, I'LL CELEBRATE VALENTINE'S DAY, TOO. I LOVE HOLIDAYS THAT MAKE YOU THROW UP!

What a Racket!

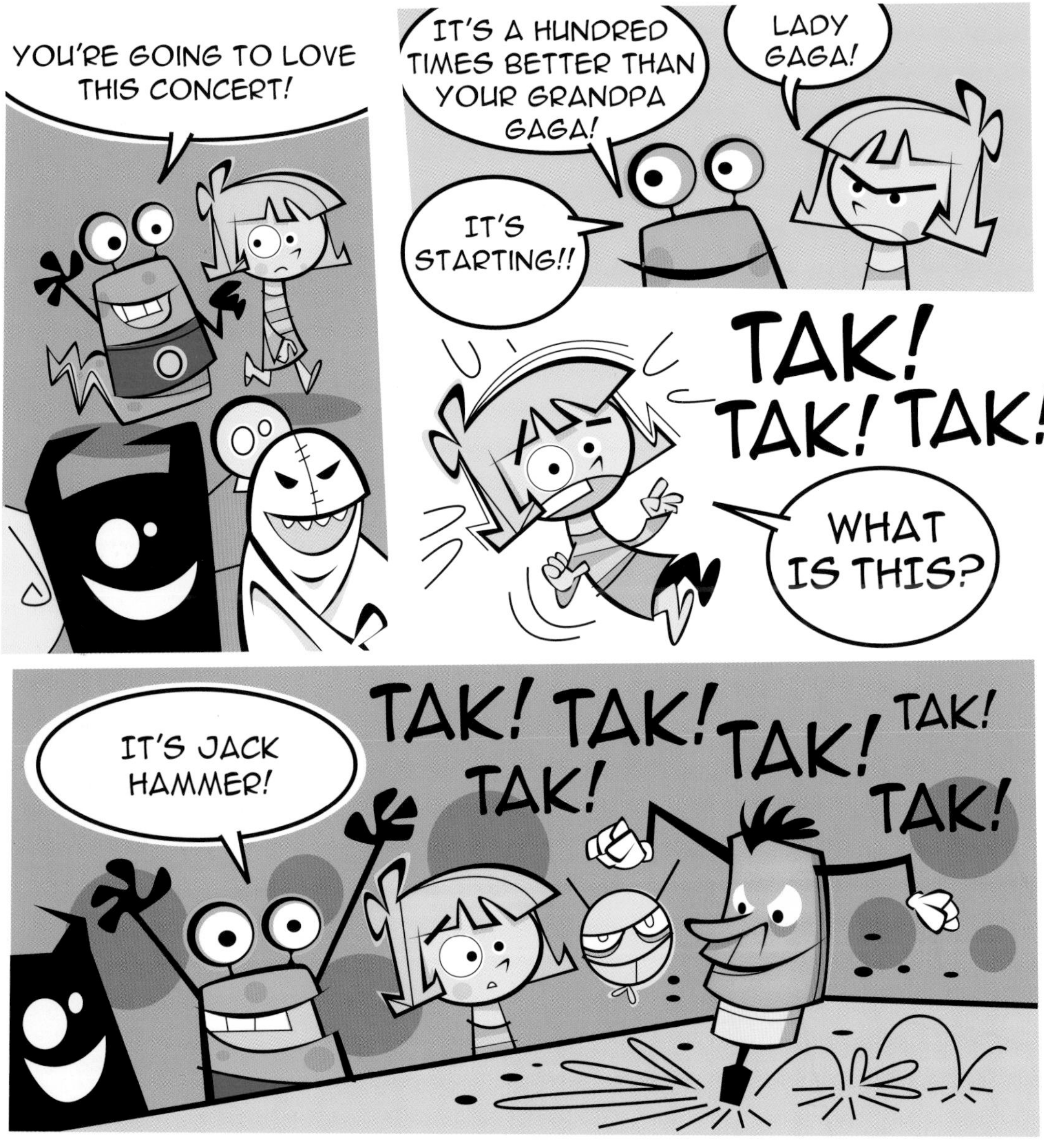

YOU'RE GOING TO LOVE THIS CONCERT!
IT'S A HUNDRED TIMES BETTER THAN YOUR GRANDPA GAGA!
LADY GAGA!
IT'S STARTING!!
TAK! TAK! TAK!
WHAT IS THIS?
IT'S JACK HAMMER!
TAK! TAK! TAK! TAK! TAK! TAK!

A Refreshing Dip

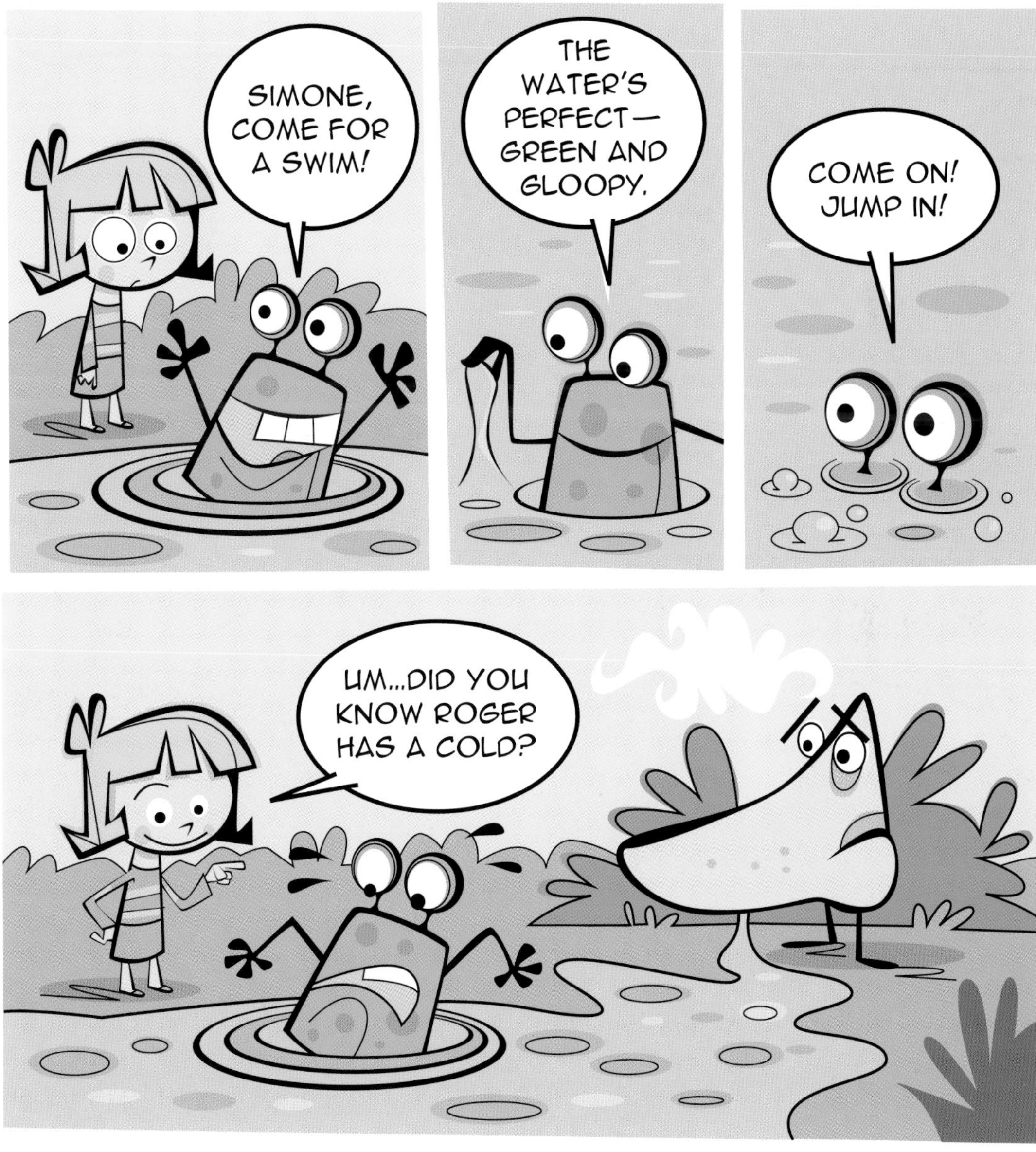
SIMONE, COME FOR A SWIM!
THE WATER'S PERFECT— GREEN AND GLOOPY.
COME ON! JUMP IN!
UM...DID YOU KNOW ROGER HAS A COLD?

The Big Bang

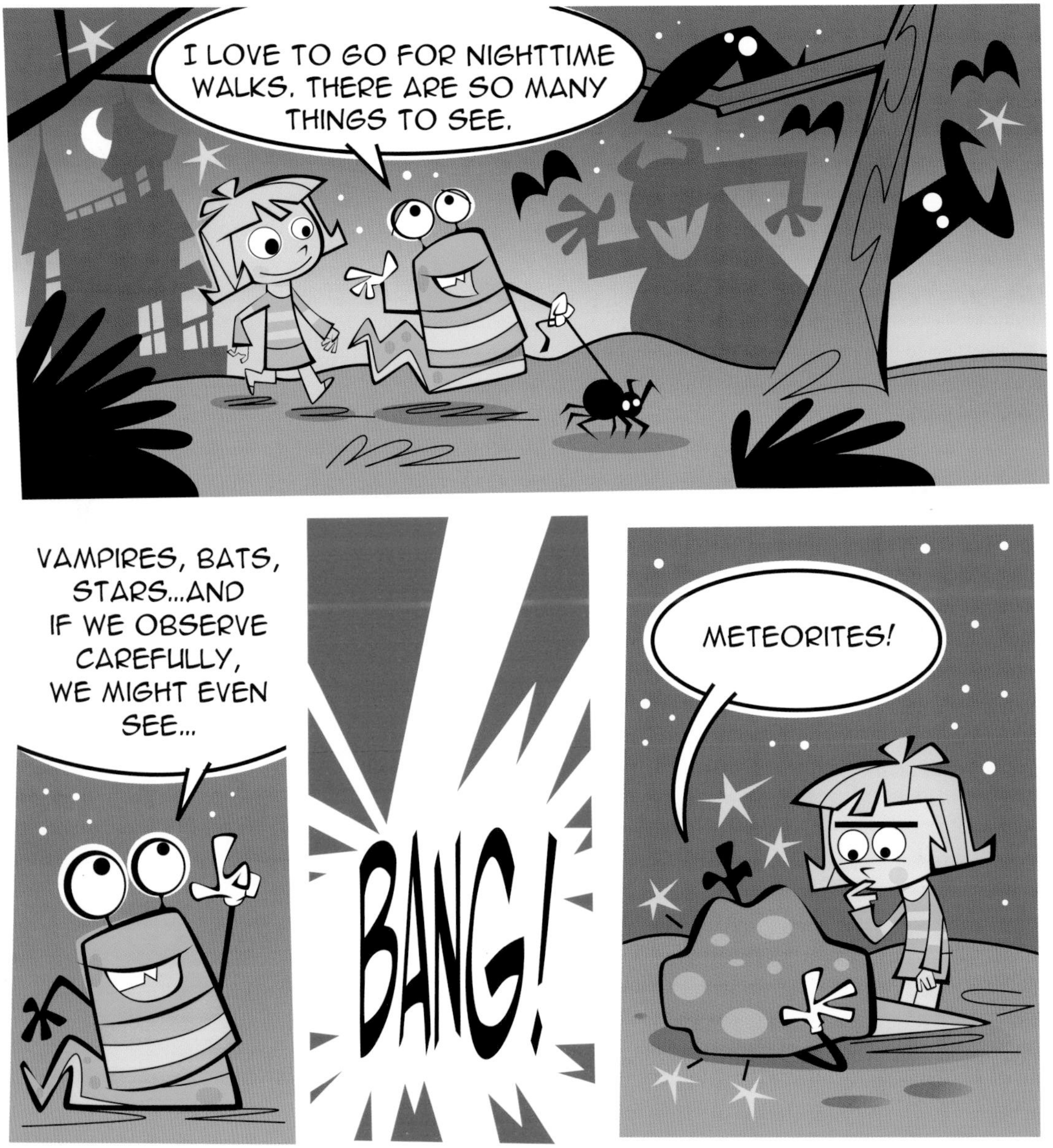
I LOVE TO GO FOR NIGHTTIME WALKS. THERE ARE SO MANY THINGS TO SEE.
VAMPIRES, BATS, STARS...AND IF WE OBSERVE CAREFULLY, WE MIGHT EVEN SEE...
BANG!
METEORITES!

Take Shelter!

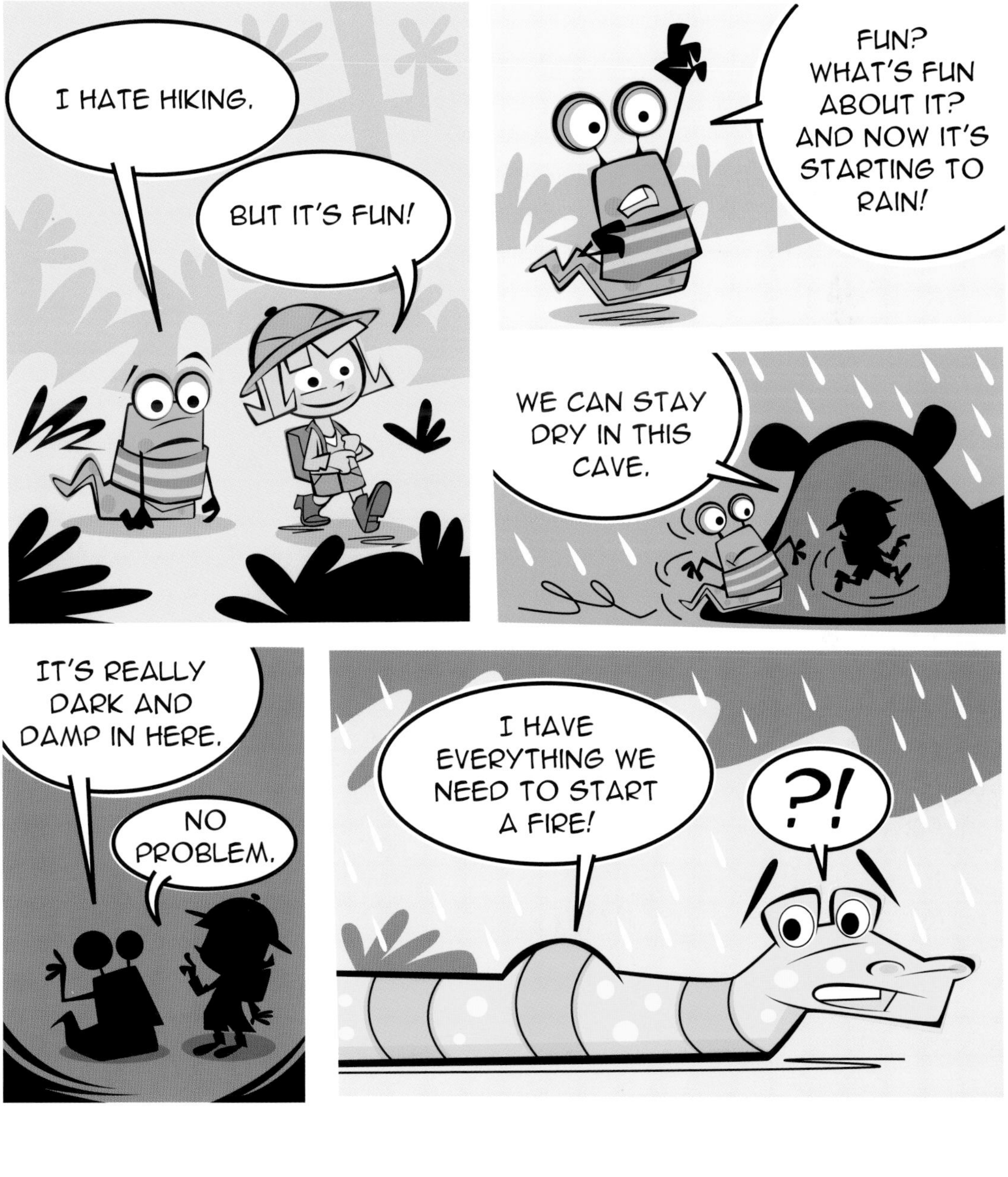
I HATE HIKING.
BUT IT'S FUN!
FUN? WHAT'S FUN ABOUT IT? AND NOW IT'S STARTING TO RAIN!
WE CAN STAY DRY IN THIS CAVE.
IT'S REALLY DARK AND DAMP IN HERE.
NO PROBLEM.
I HAVE EVERYTHING WE NEED TO START A FIRE!
?!

Back to School

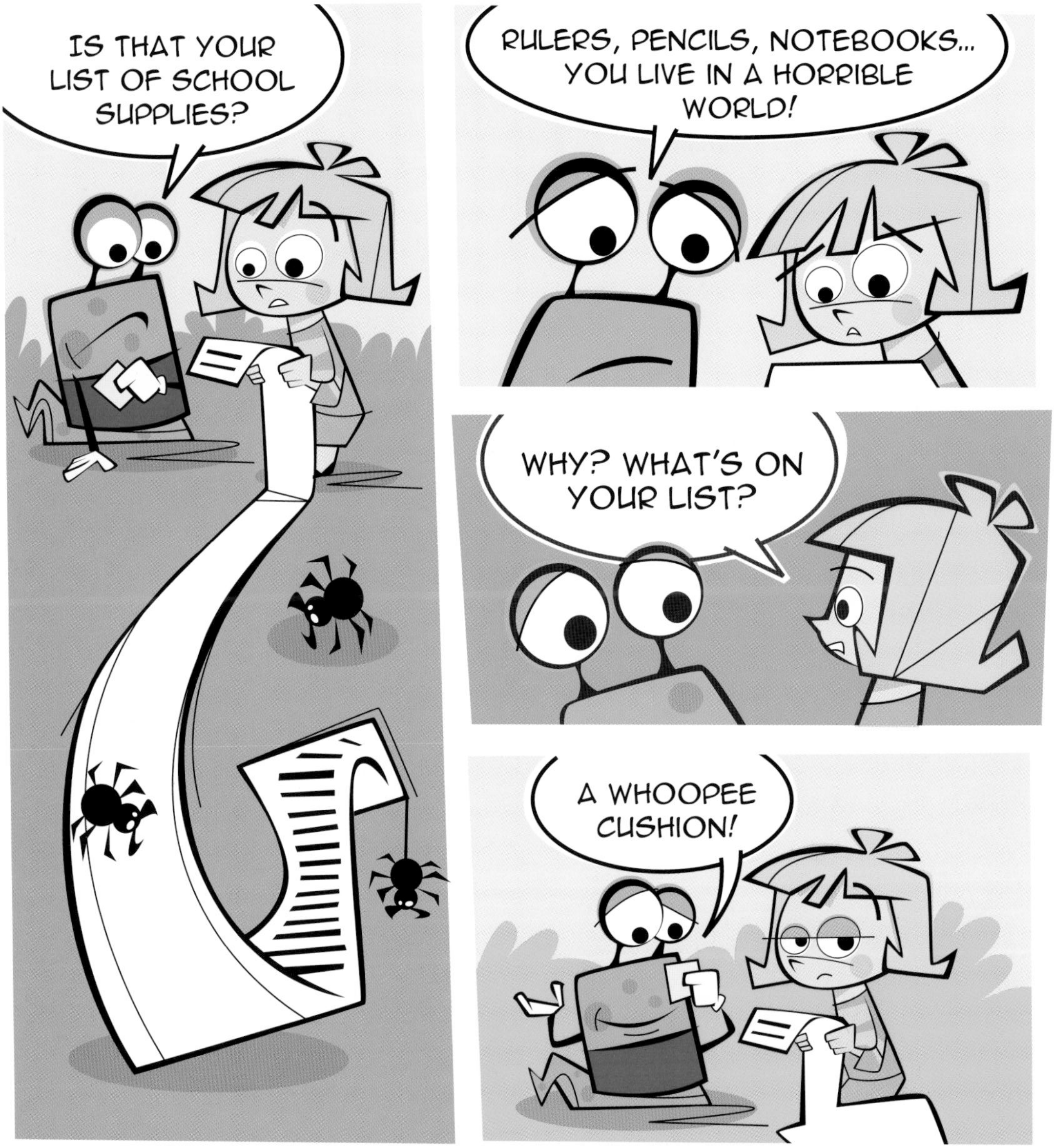
IS THAT YOUR LIST OF SCHOOL SUPPLIES?
RULERS, PENCILS, NOTEBOOKS... YOU LIVE IN A HORRIBLE WORLD!
WHY? WHAT'S ON YOUR LIST?
A WHOOPEE CUSHION!

With Friends Like These

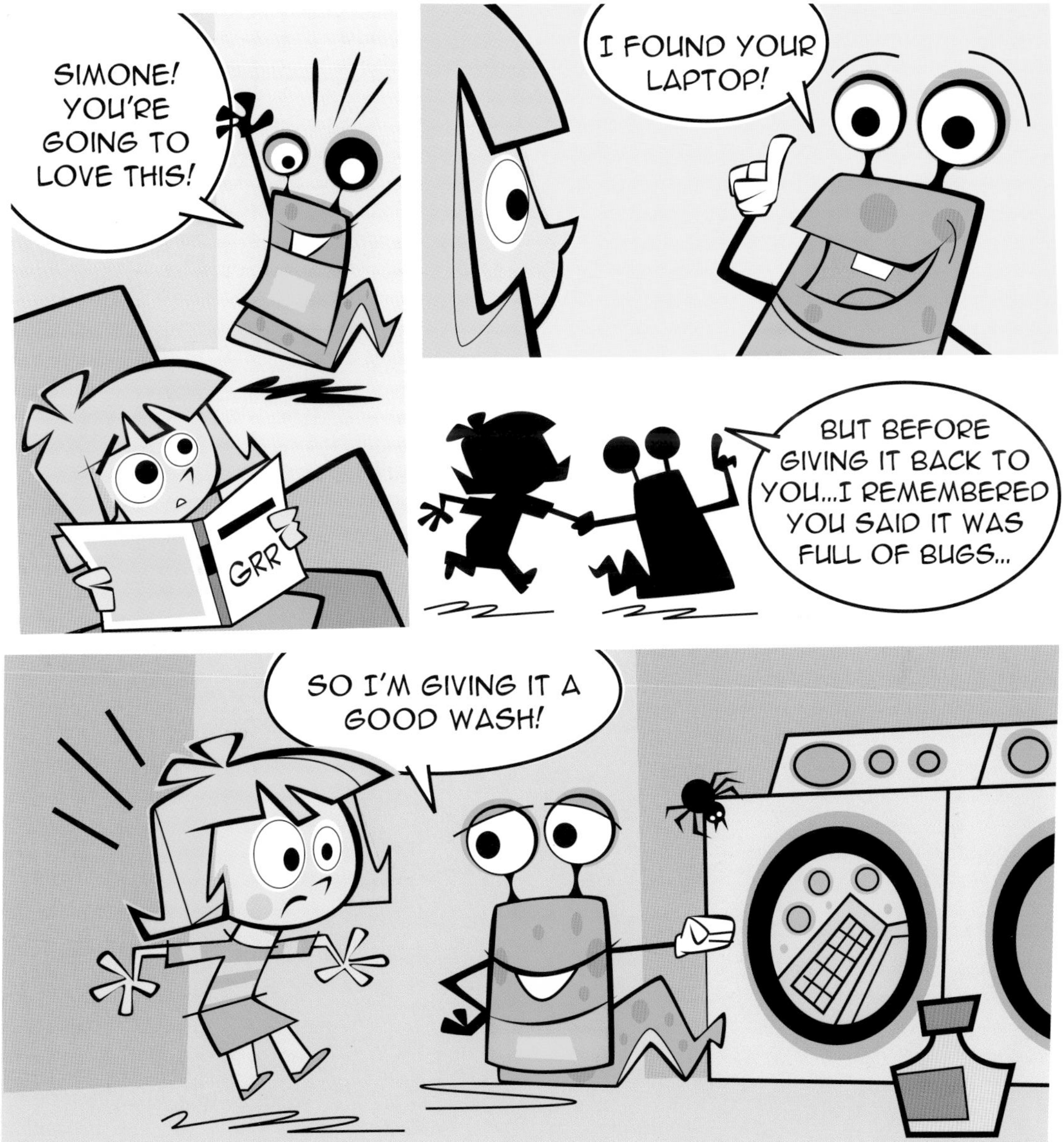

SIMONE! YOU'RE GOING TO LOVE THIS!
GRR
I FOUND YOUR LAPTOP!
BUT BEFORE GIVING IT BACK TO YOU...I REMEMBERED YOU SAID IT WAS FULL OF BUGS...
SO I'M GIVING IT A GOOD WASH!

The Chase Is On!

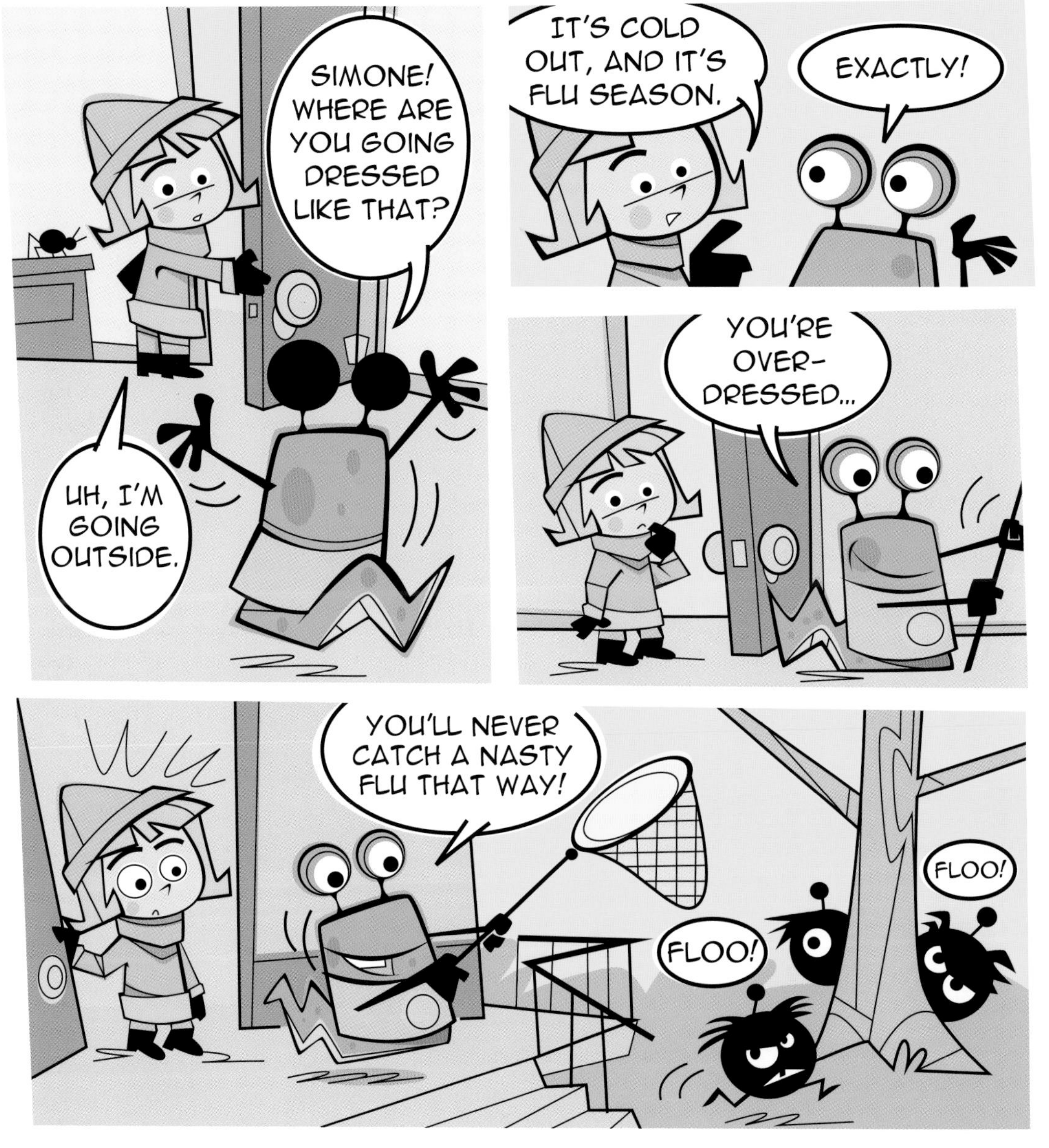

SIMONE! WHERE ARE YOU GOING DRESSED LIKE THAT?
UH, I'M GOING OUTSIDE.
IT'S COLD OUT, AND IT'S FLU SEASON.
EXACTLY!
YOU'RE OVER-DRESSED...
YOU'LL NEVER CATCH A NASTY FLU THAT WAY!
FLOO!
FLOO!

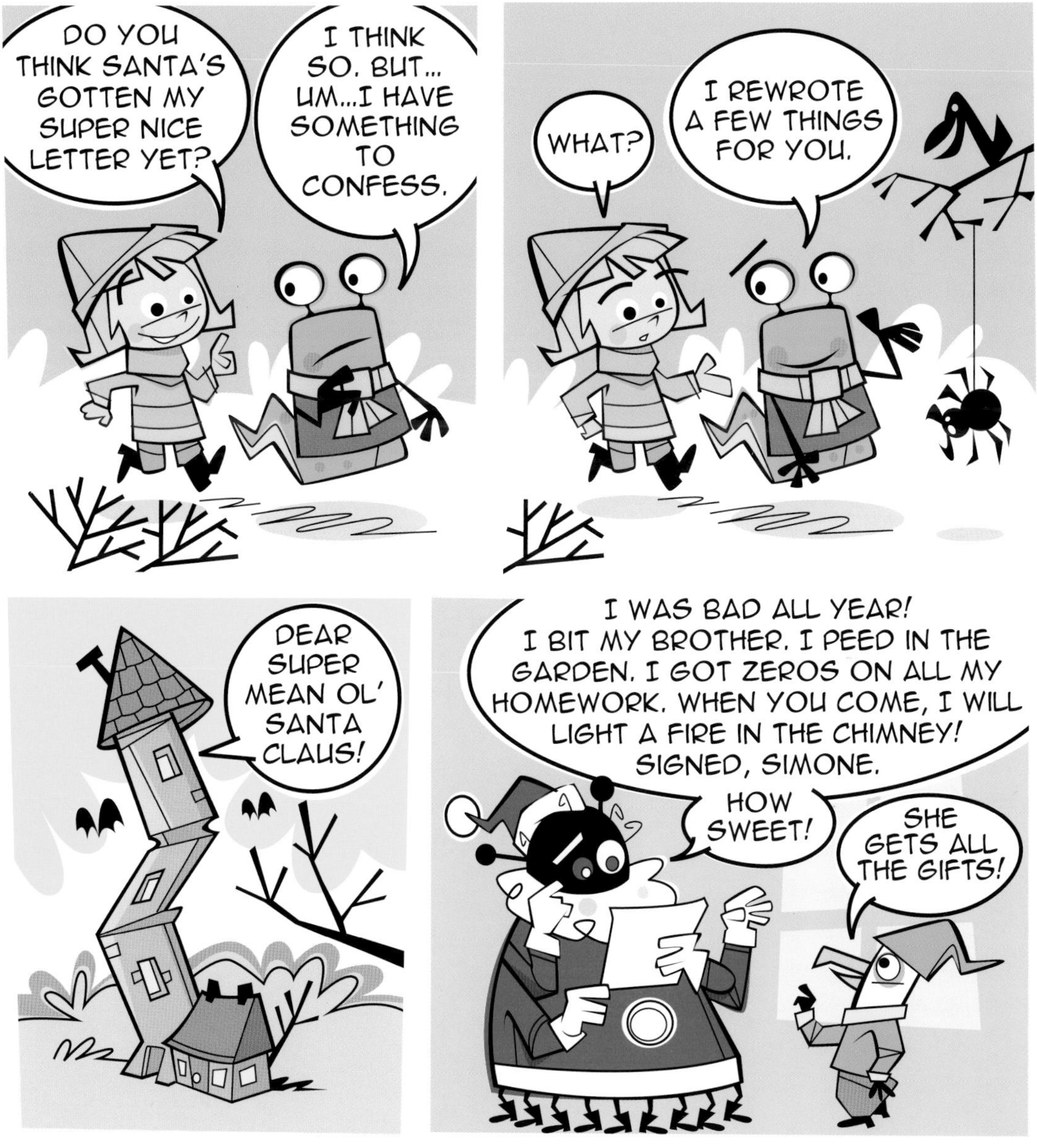
DO YOU THINK SANTA'S GOTTEN MY SUPER NICE LETTER YET?
I THINK SO. BUT... UM...I HAVE SOMETHING TO CONFESS.
WHAT?
I REWROTE A FEW THINGS FOR YOU.
DEAR SUPER MEAN OL' SANTA CLAUS!
I WAS BAD ALL YEAR! I BIT MY BROTHER. I PEED IN THE GARDEN. I GOT ZEROS ON ALL MY HOMEWORK. WHEN YOU COME, I WILL LIGHT A FIRE IN THE CHIMNEY! SIGNED, SIMONE.
HOW SWEET!
SHE GETS ALL THE GIFTS!

It's a Strike!

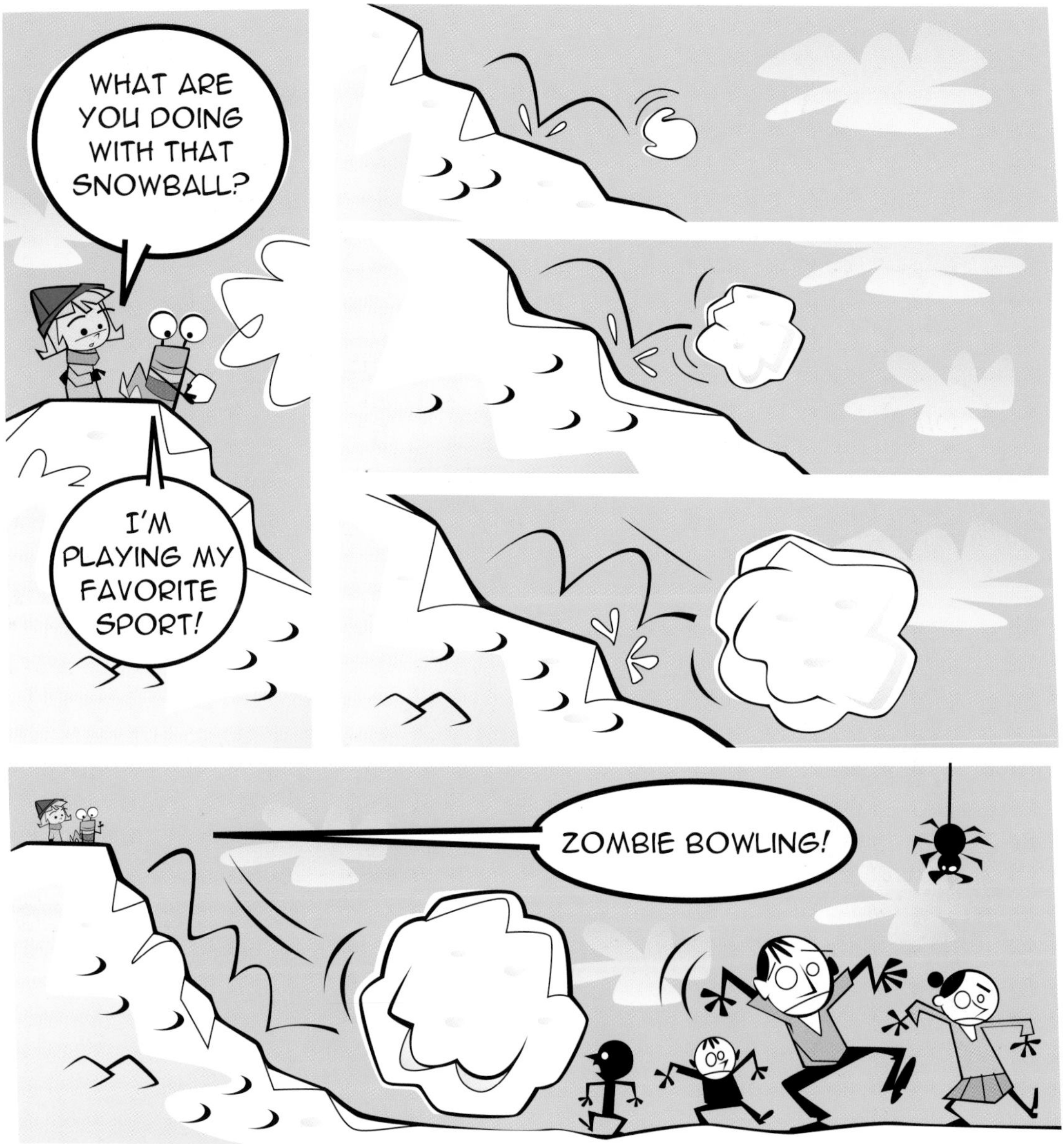

WHAT ARE YOU DOING WITH THAT SNOWBALL?
I'M PLAYING MY FAVORITE SPORT!
ZOMBIE BOWLING!

Catch Me If You Can!

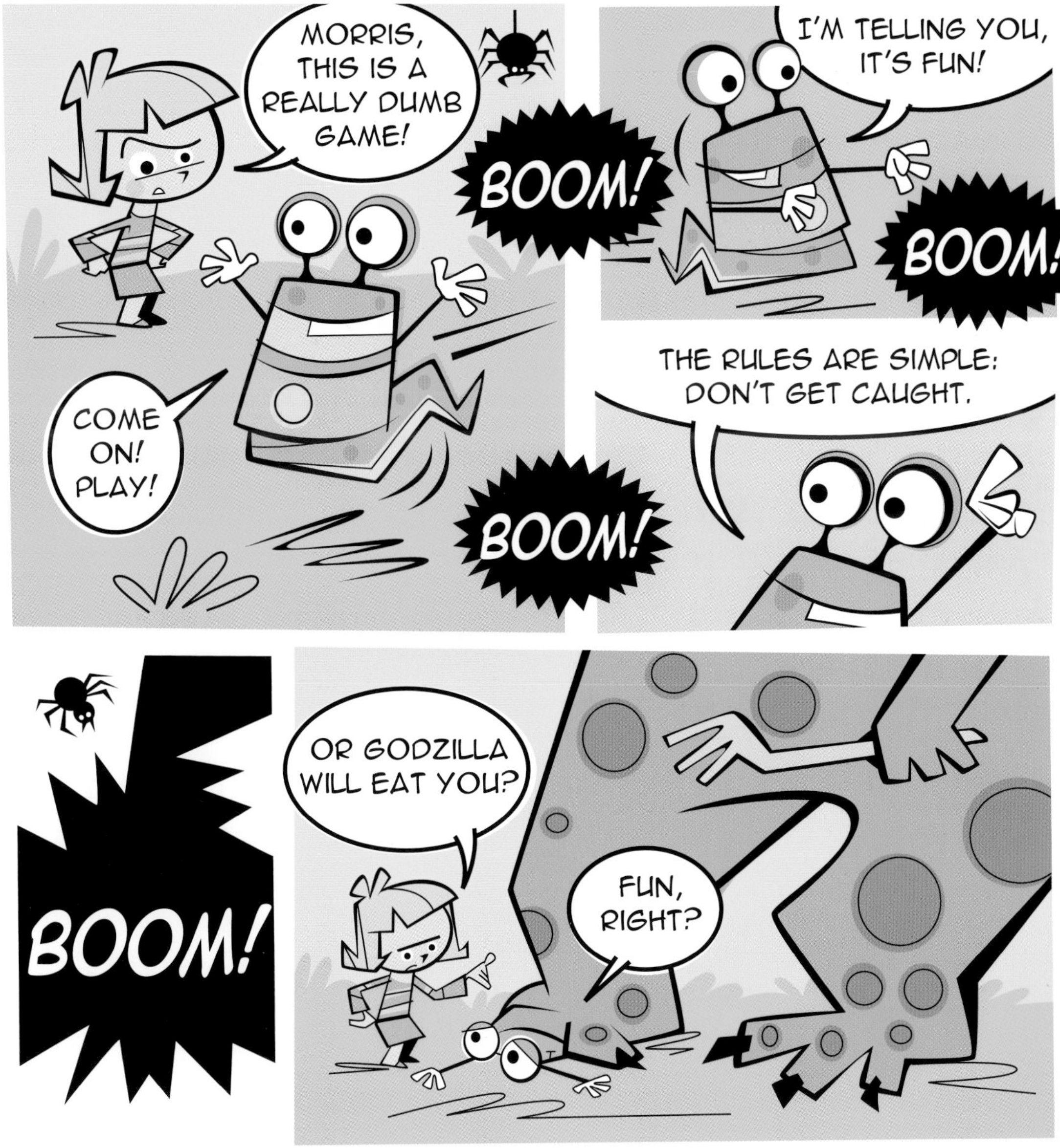
MORRIS, THIS IS A REALLY DUMB GAME!
COME ON! PLAY!
BOOM!
BOOM!
I'M TELLING YOU, IT'S FUN!
BOOM!
THE RULES ARE SIMPLE: DON'T GET CAUGHT.
BOOM!
OR GODZILLA WILL EAT YOU?
FUN, RIGHT?

Hitting Birdies

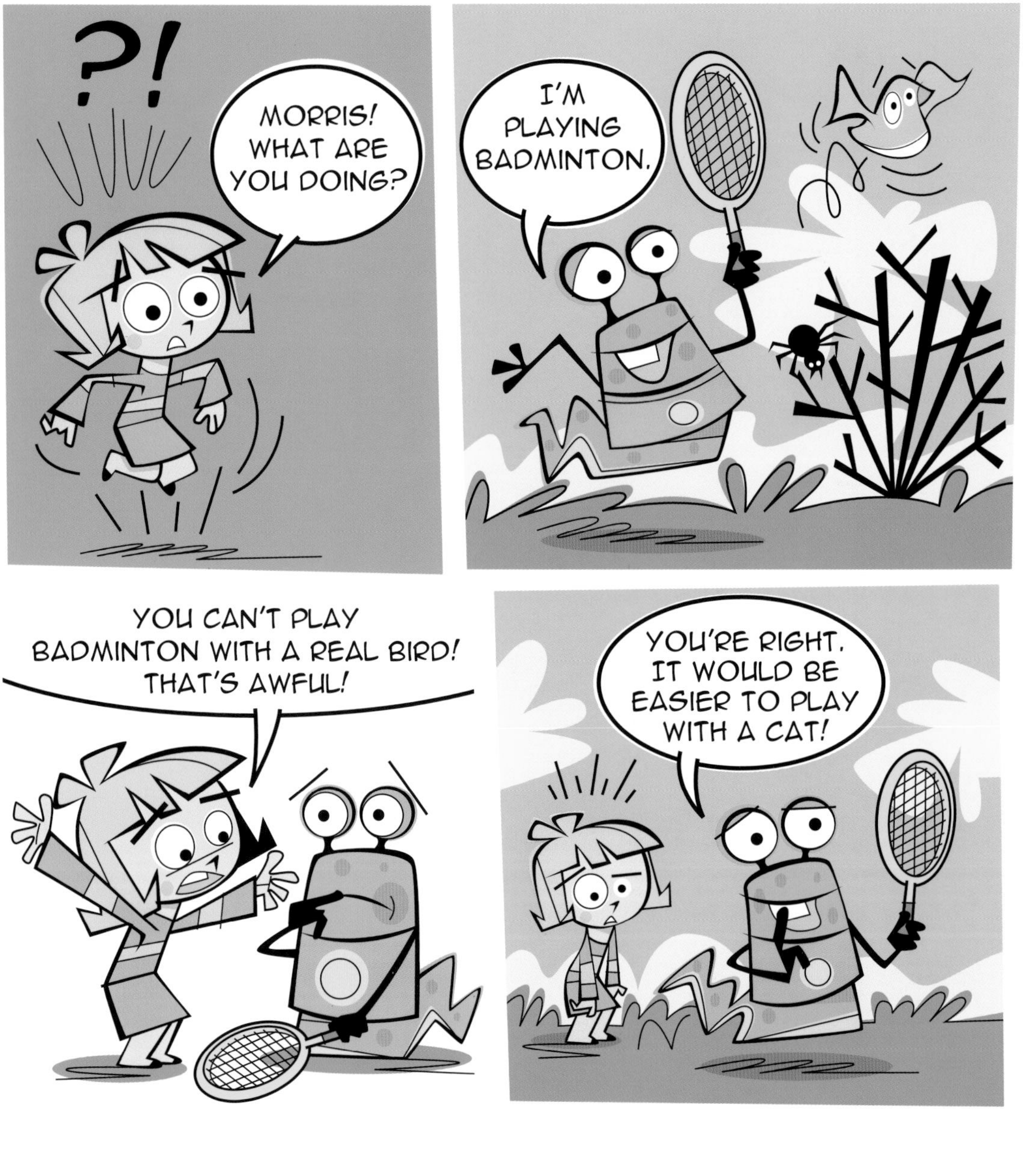

?!
MORRIS! WHAT ARE YOU DOING?
I'M PLAYING BADMINTON.
YOU CAN'T PLAY BADMINTON WITH A REAL BIRD! THAT'S AWFUL!
YOU'RE RIGHT. IT WOULD BE EASIER TO PLAY WITH A CAT!

Heavyweight

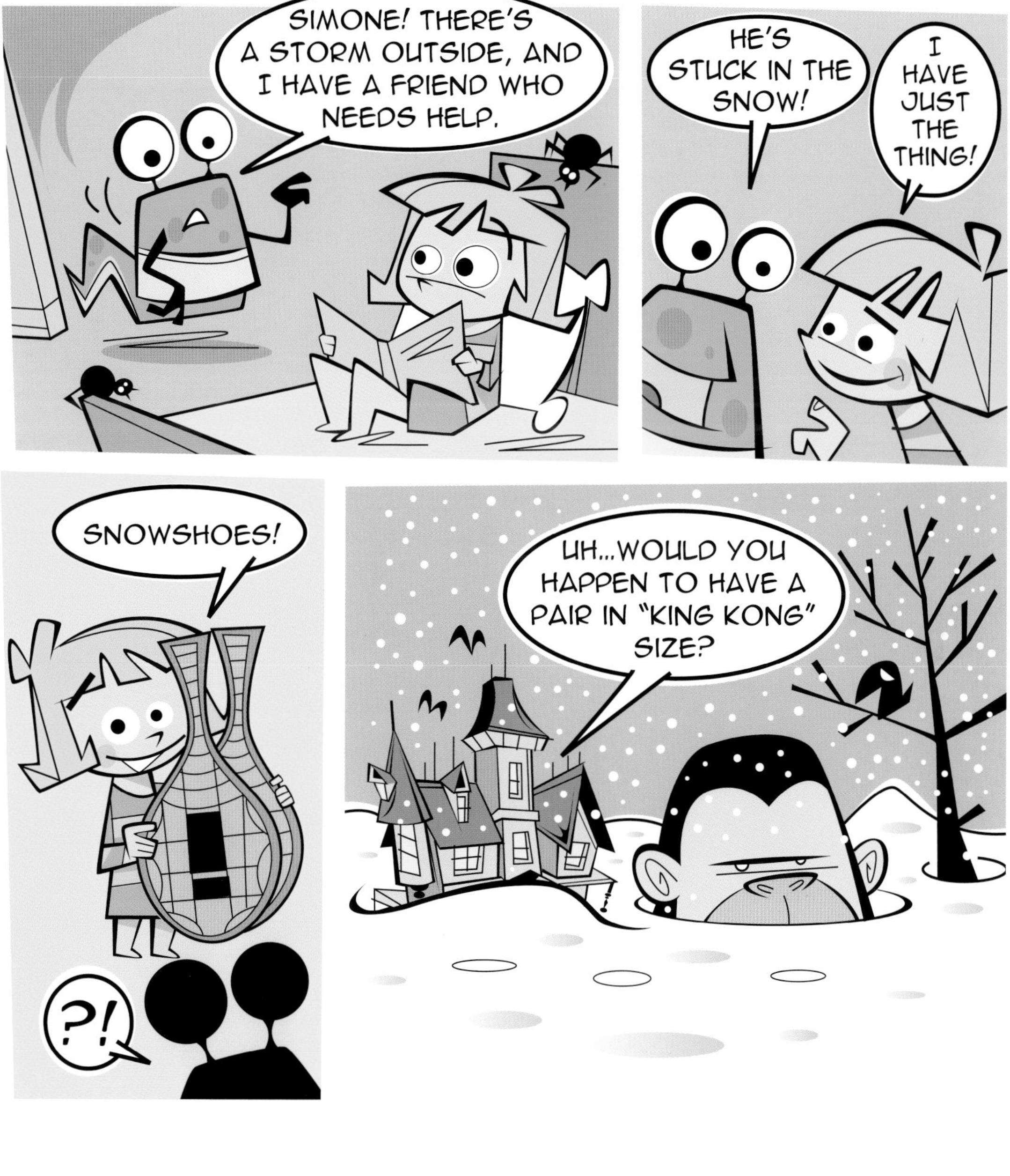
SIMONE! THERE'S A STORM OUTSIDE, AND I HAVE A FRIEND WHO NEEDS HELP.
HE'S STUCK IN THE SNOW!
I HAVE JUST THE THING!
SNOWSHOES!
?!
UH...WOULD YOU HAPPEN TO HAVE A PAIR IN "KING KONG" SIZE?

A Lot of Noise for Nothing...

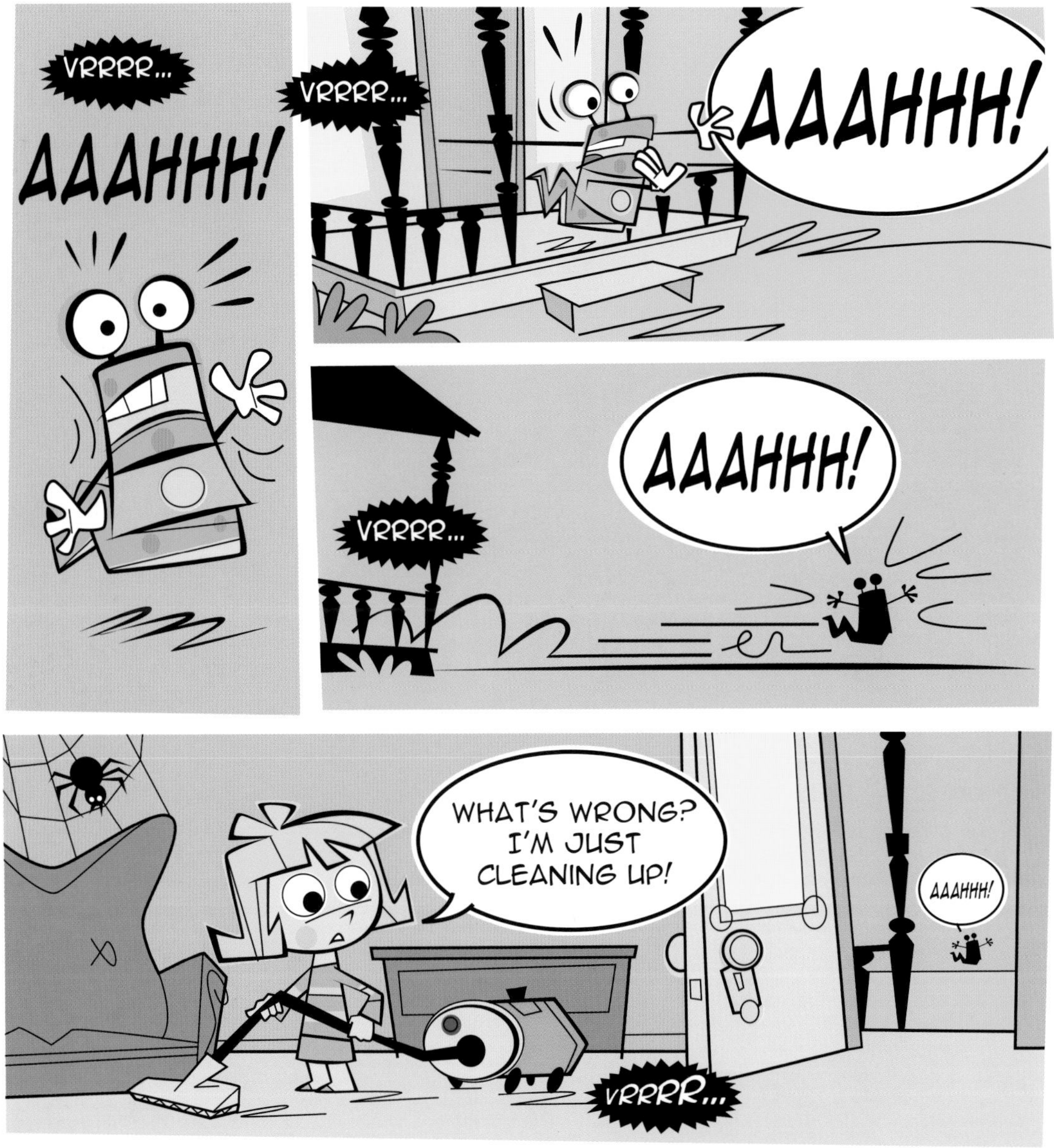
VRRRR...
AAAHHH!
VRRRR...
AAAHHH!
VRRRR...
AAAHHH!
WHAT'S WRONG? I'M JUST CLEANING UP!
AAAHHH!
VRRRR...

Suppertime!

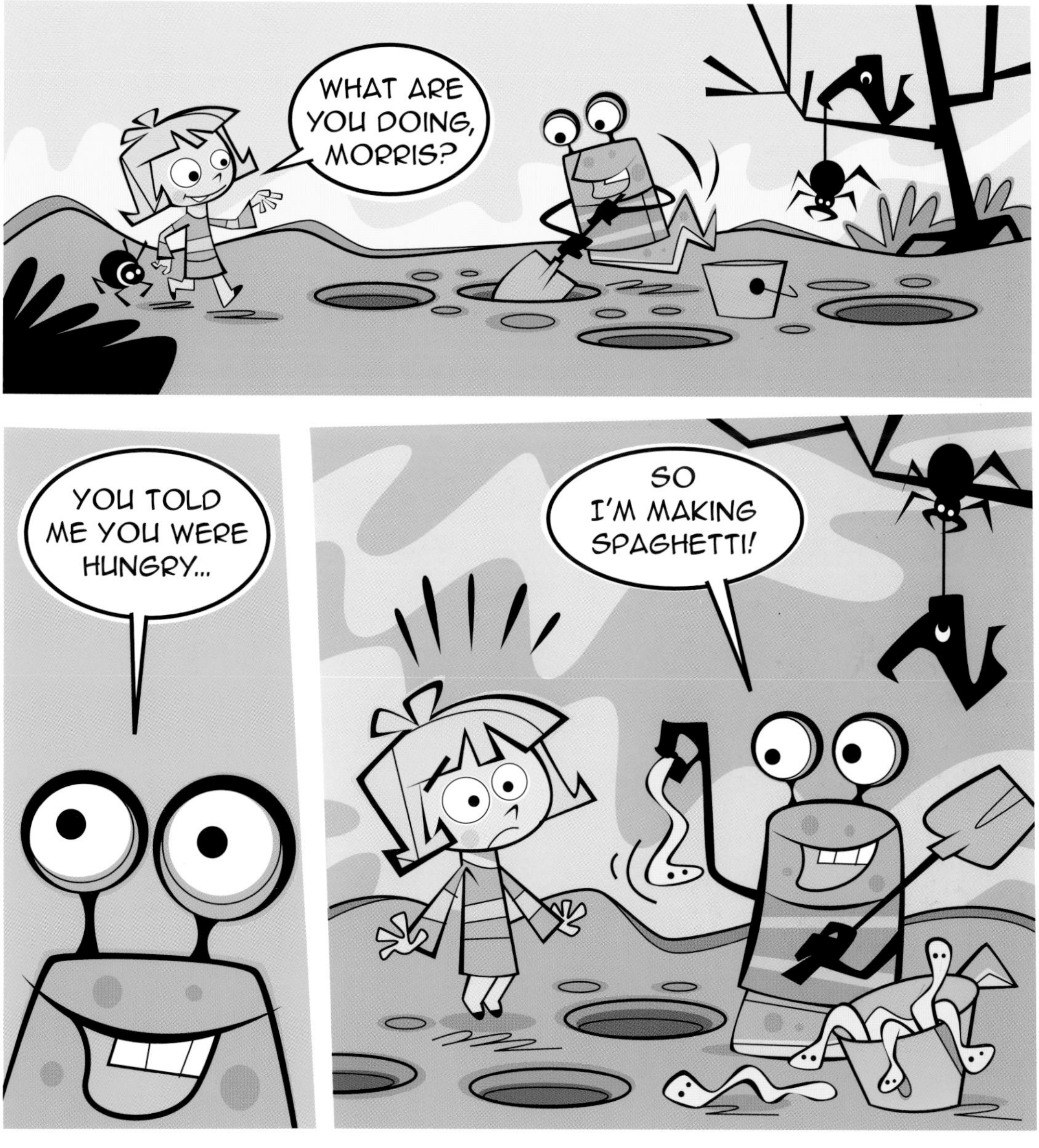
WHAT ARE YOU DOING, MORRIS?
YOU TOLD ME YOU WERE HUNGRY...
SO I'M MAKING SPAGHETTI!

Frightful Weather

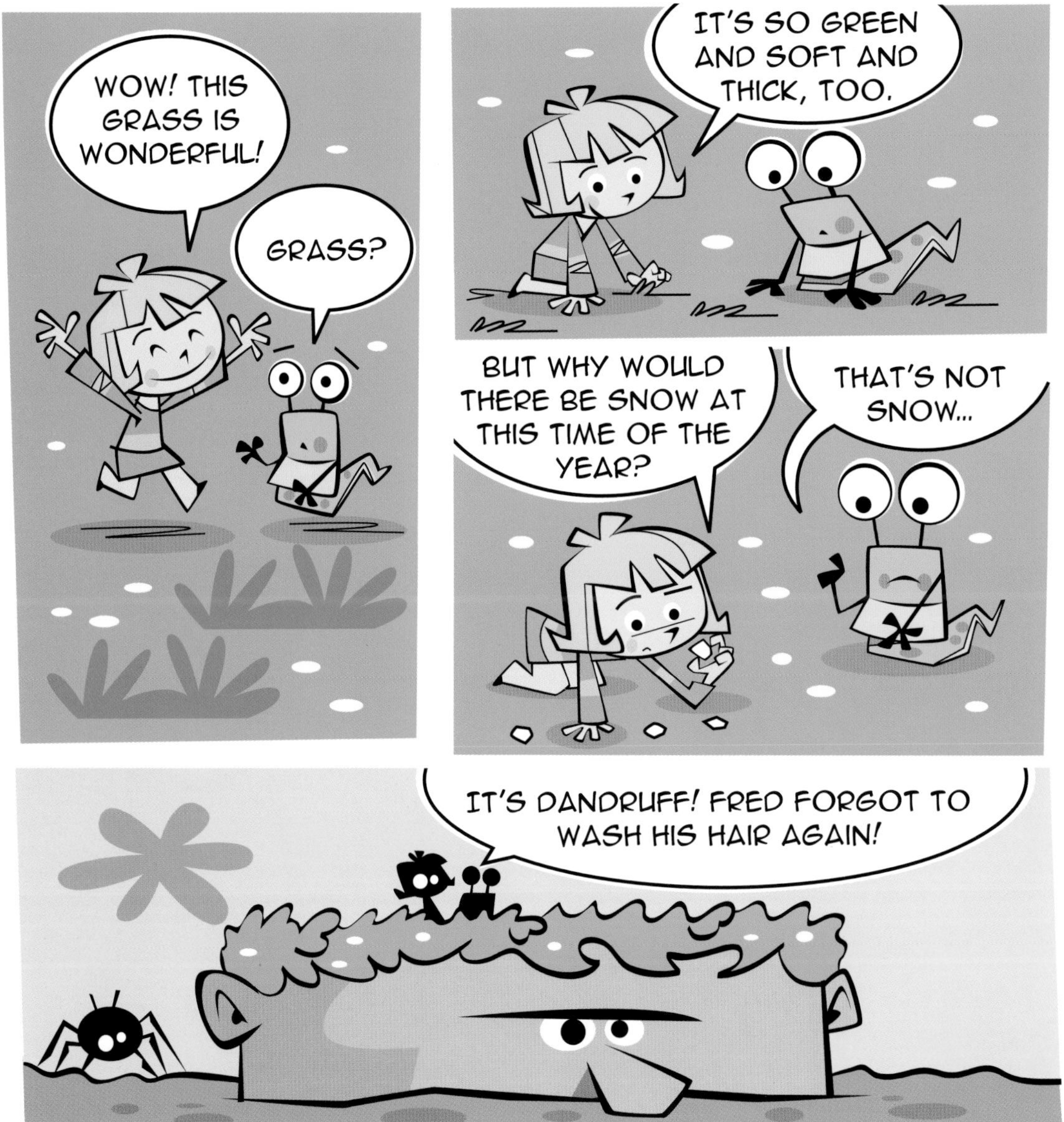
WOW! THIS GRASS IS WONDERFUL!
GRASS?
IT'S SO GREEN AND SOFT AND THICK, TOO.
BUT WHY WOULD THERE BE SNOW AT THIS TIME OF THE YEAR?
THAT'S NOT SNOW...
IT'S DANDRUFF! FRED FORGOT TO WASH HIS HAIR AGAIN!

It's the Price You Pay

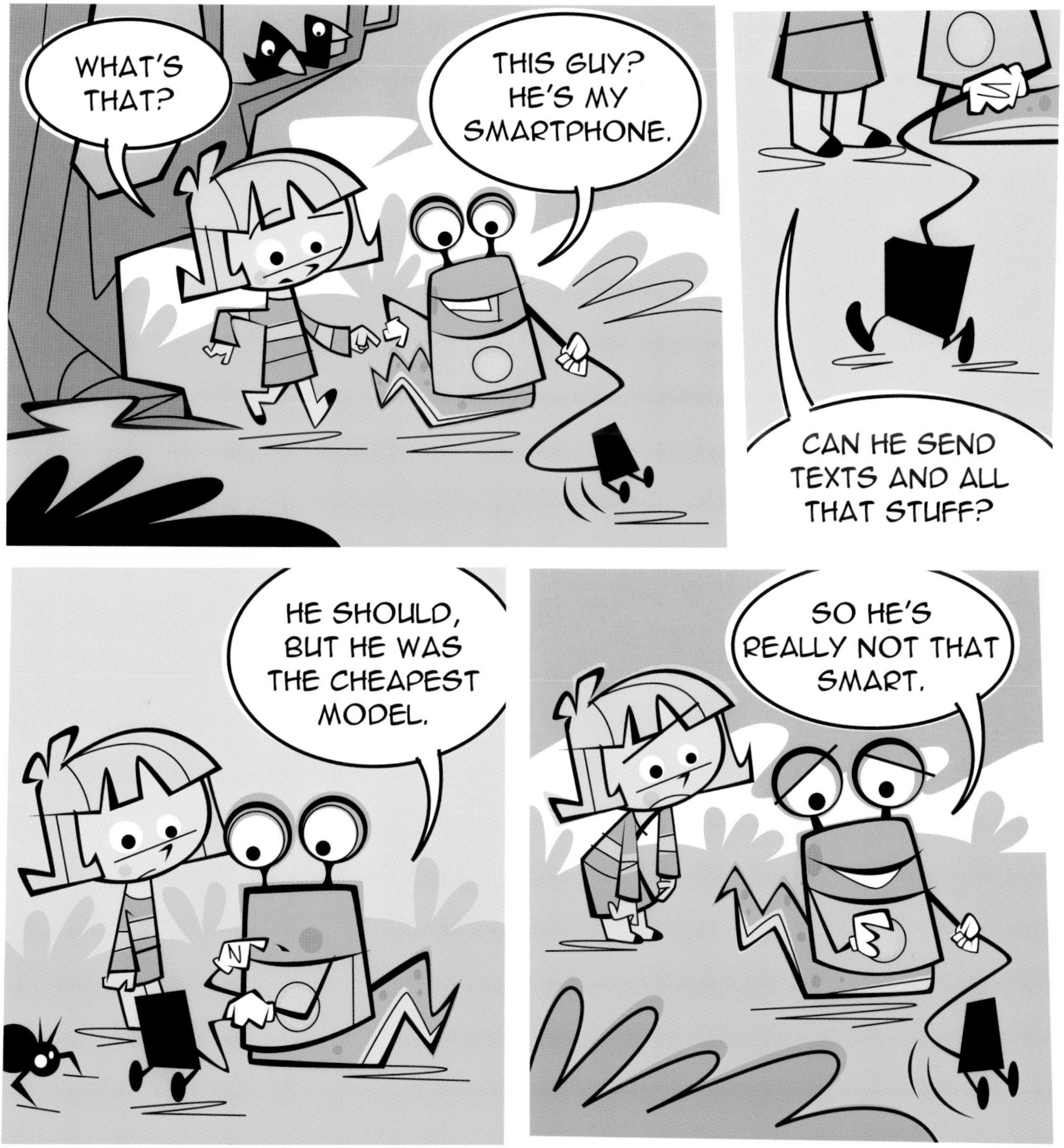
WHAT'S THAT?
THIS GUY? HE'S MY SMARTPHONE.
CAN HE SEND TEXTS AND ALL THAT STUFF?
HE SHOULD, BUT HE WAS THE CHEAPEST MODEL.
SO HE'S REALLY NOT THAT SMART.

Pretty Scary

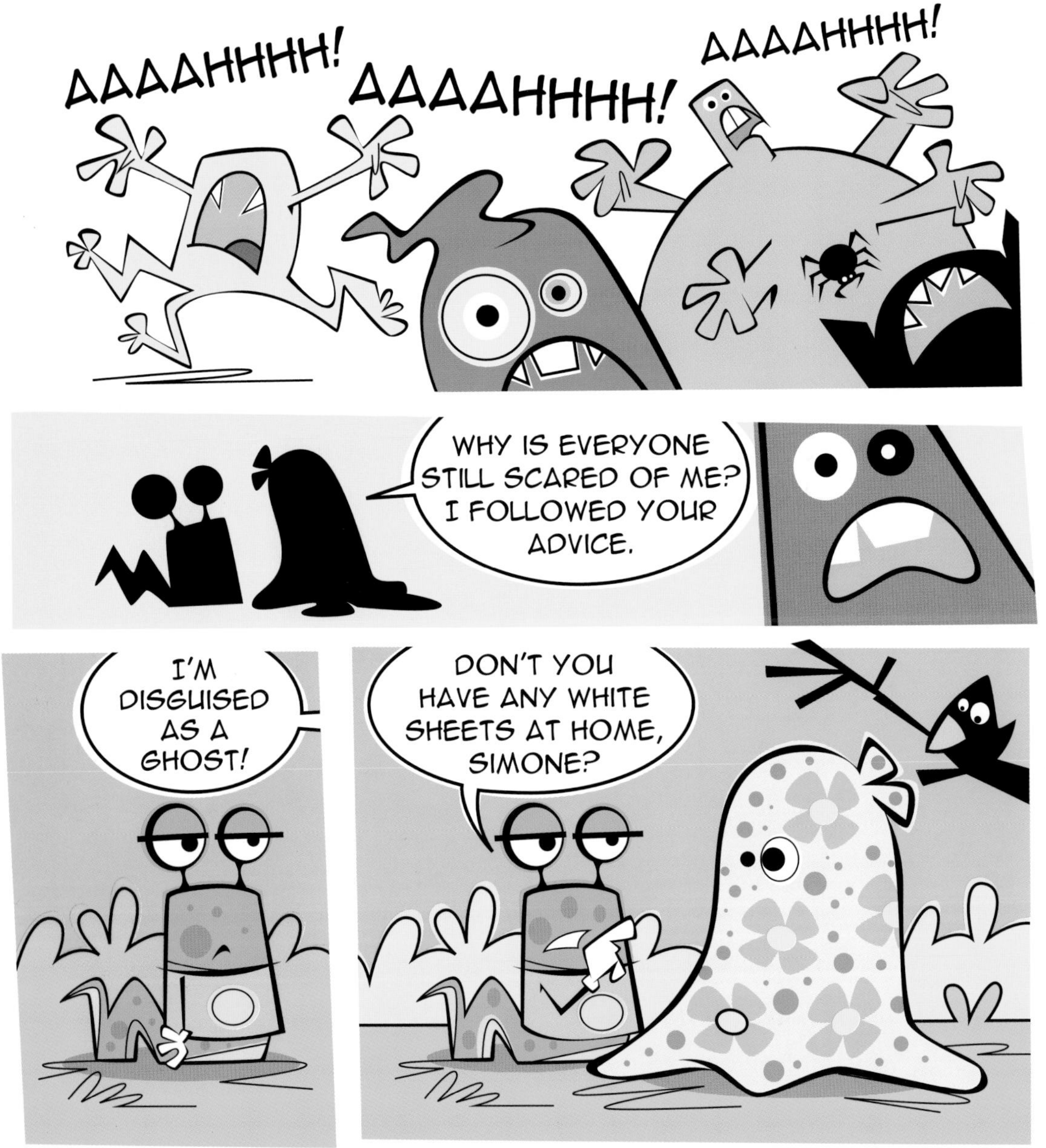
AAAAHHHH!
AAAAHHHH!
AAAAHHHH!
WHY IS EVERYONE STILL SCARED OF ME? I FOLLOWED YOUR ADVICE.
I'M DISGUISED AS A GHOST!
DON'T YOU HAVE ANY WHITE SHEETS AT HOME, SIMONE?

Just the Thing!

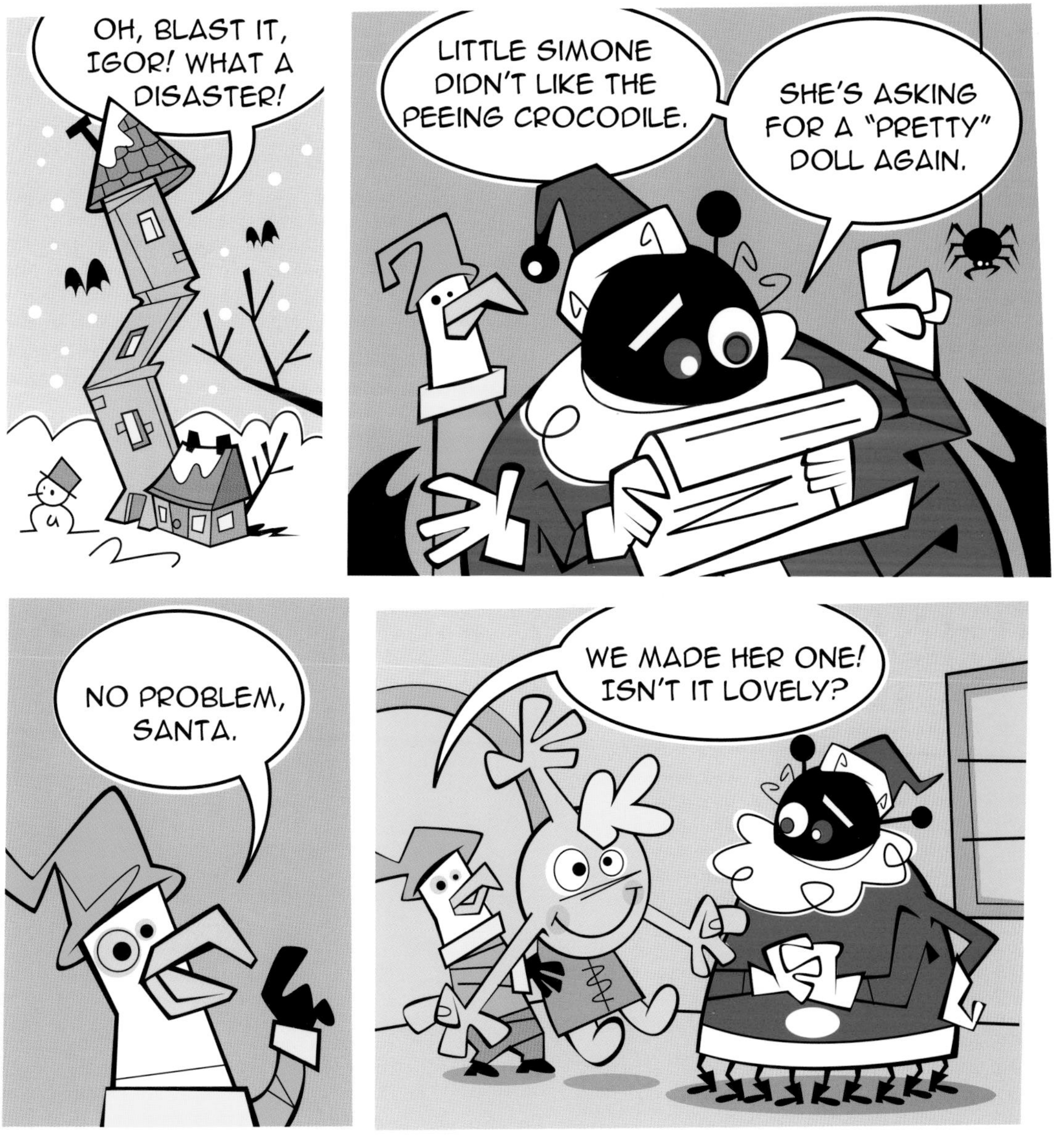
OH, BLAST IT, IGOR! WHAT A DISASTER!
LITTLE SIMONE DIDN'T LIKE THE PEEING CROCODILE.
SHE'S ASKING FOR A "PRETTY" DOLL AGAIN.
NO PROBLEM, SANTA.
WE MADE HER ONE! ISN'T IT LOVELY?

Tiny Guest List

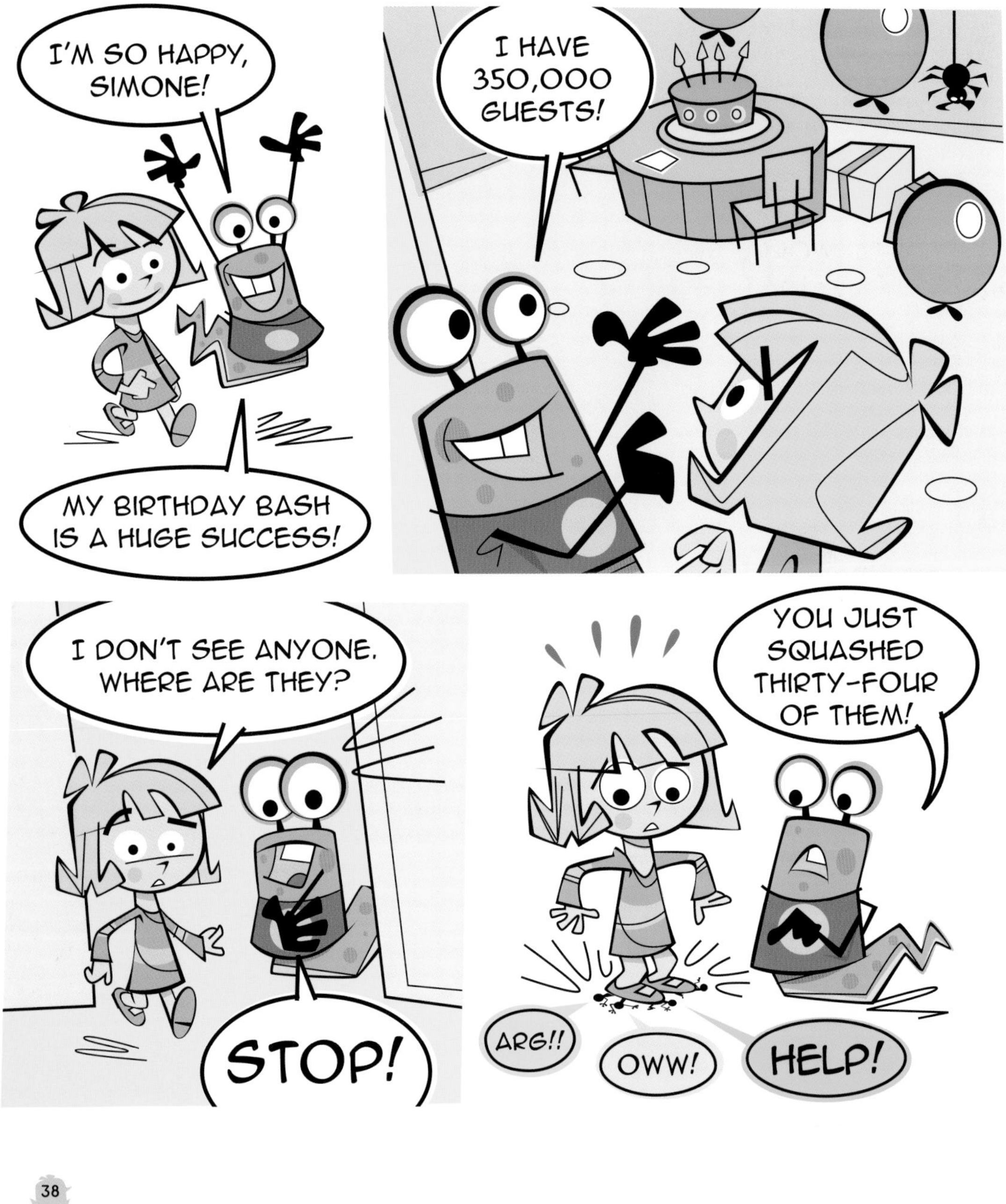

I'M SO HAPPY, SIMONE!
MY BIRTHDAY BASH IS A HUGE SUCCESS!
I HAVE 350,000 GUESTS!
I DON'T SEE ANYONE. WHERE ARE THEY?
STOP!
YOU JUST SQUASHED THIRTY-FOUR OF THEM!
ARG!!
OWW!
HELP!

Yum!

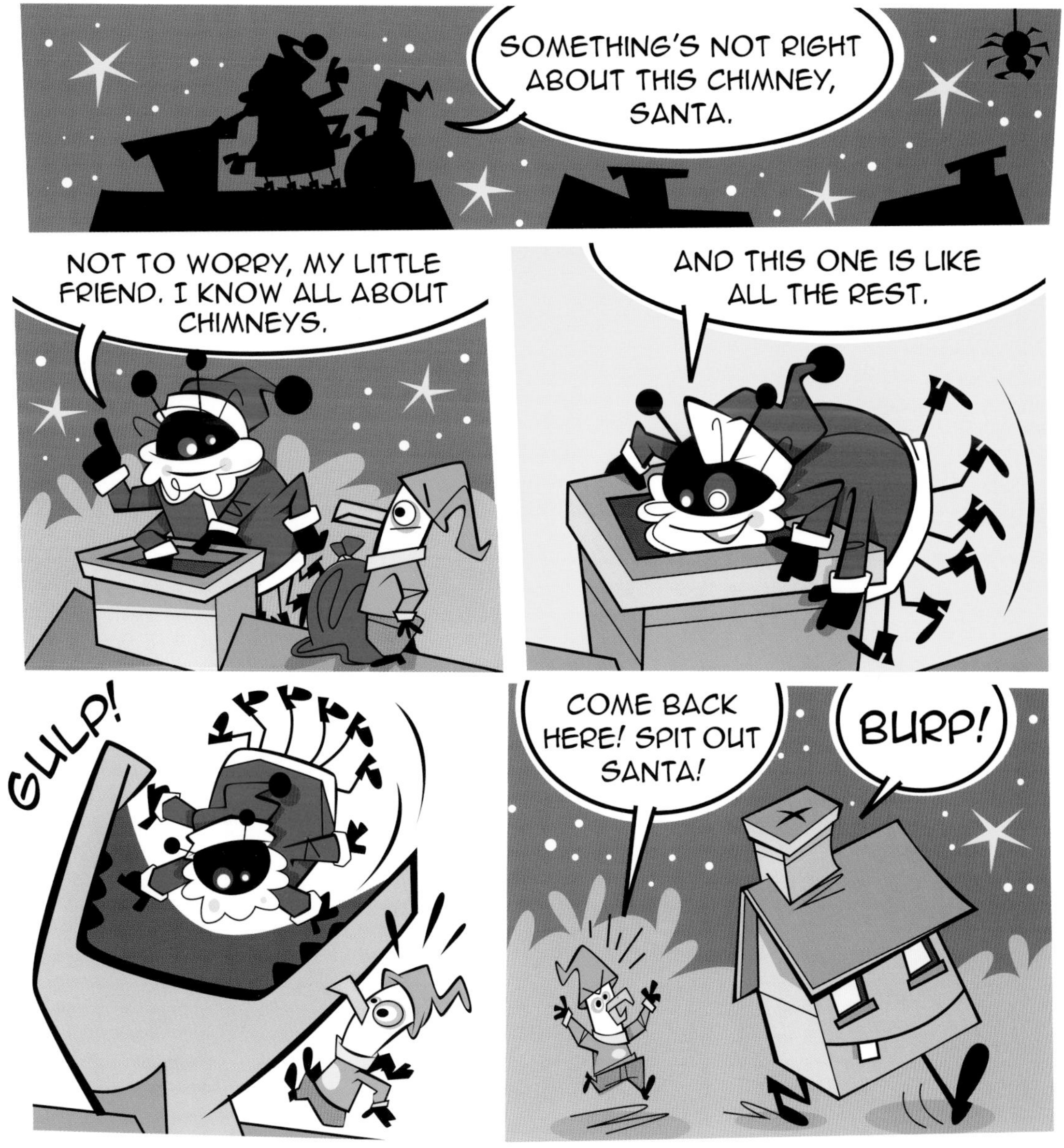

SOMETHING'S NOT RIGHT ABOUT THIS CHIMNEY, SANTA.
NOT TO WORRY, MY LITTLE FRIEND. I KNOW ALL ABOUT CHIMNEYS.
AND THIS ONE IS LIKE ALL THE REST.
GULP!
COME BACK HERE! SPIT OUT SANTA!
BURP!

A Surprise to Boot

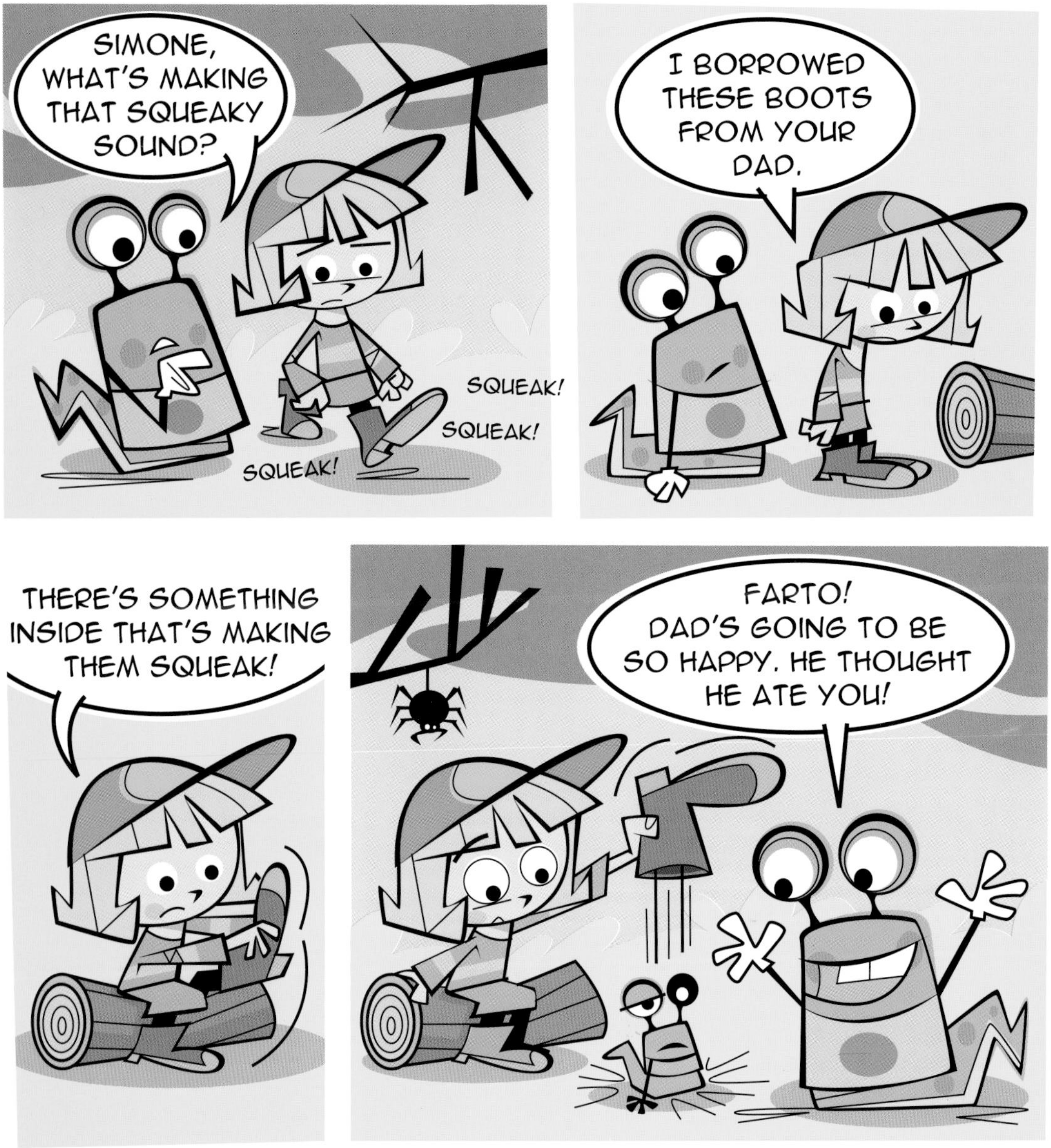
SIMONE, WHAT'S MAKING THAT SQUEAKY SOUND?
SQUEAK!
SQUEAK!
SQUEAK!
I BORROWED THESE BOOTS FROM YOUR DAD.
THERE'S SOMETHING INSIDE THAT'S MAKING THEM SQUEAK!
FARTO! DAD'S GOING TO BE SO HAPPY. HE THOUGHT HE ATE YOU!

Take Your Medicine

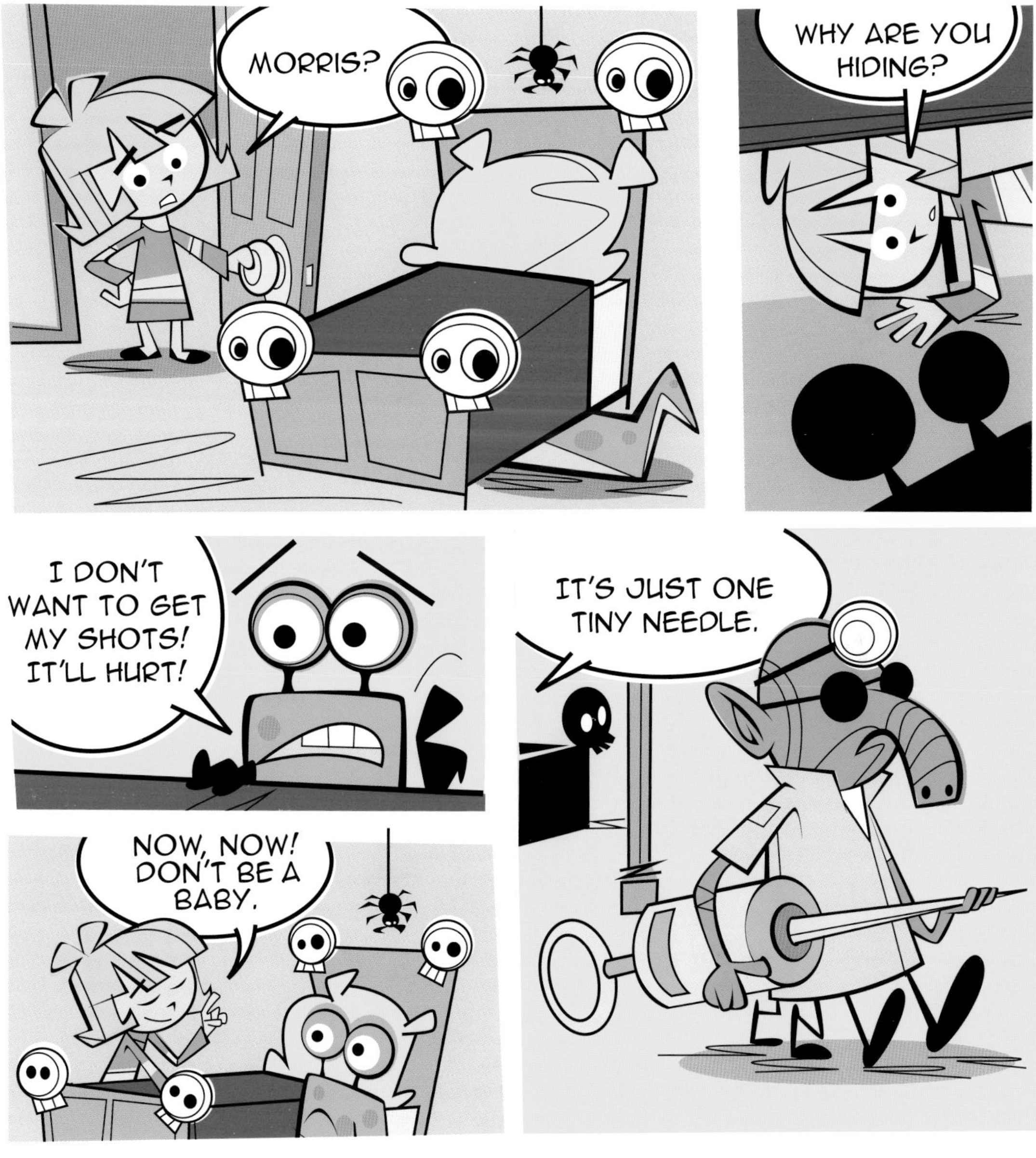

MORRIS?
WHY ARE YOU HIDING?
I DON'T WANT TO GET MY SHOTS! IT'LL HURT!
NOW, NOW! DON'T BE A BABY.
IT'S JUST ONE TINY NEEDLE.

Game, Set, Match!

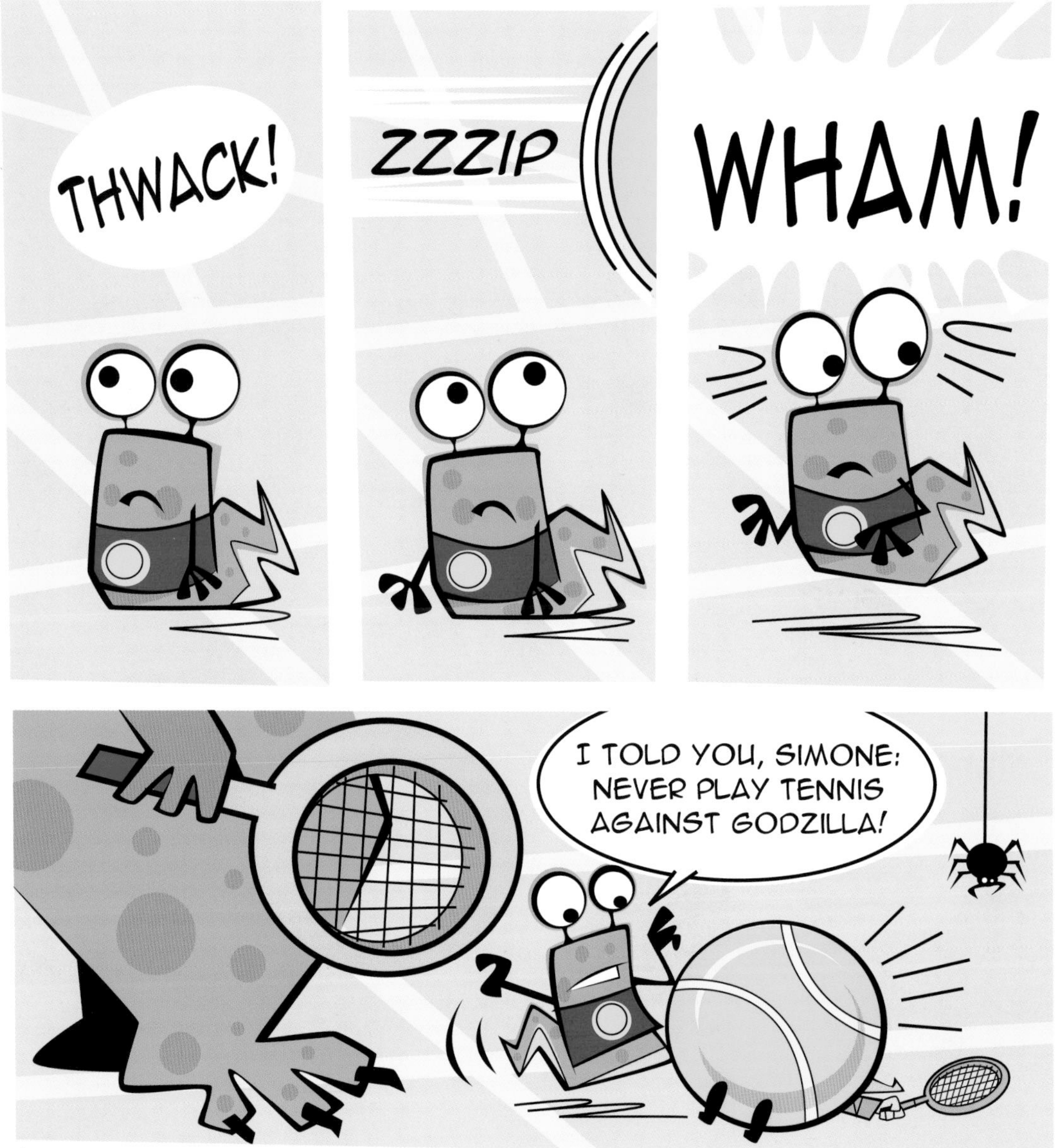
THWACK!
ZZZIP
WHAM!
I TOLD YOU, SIMONE: NEVER PLAY TENNIS AGAINST GODZILLA!

When You Gotta Go...

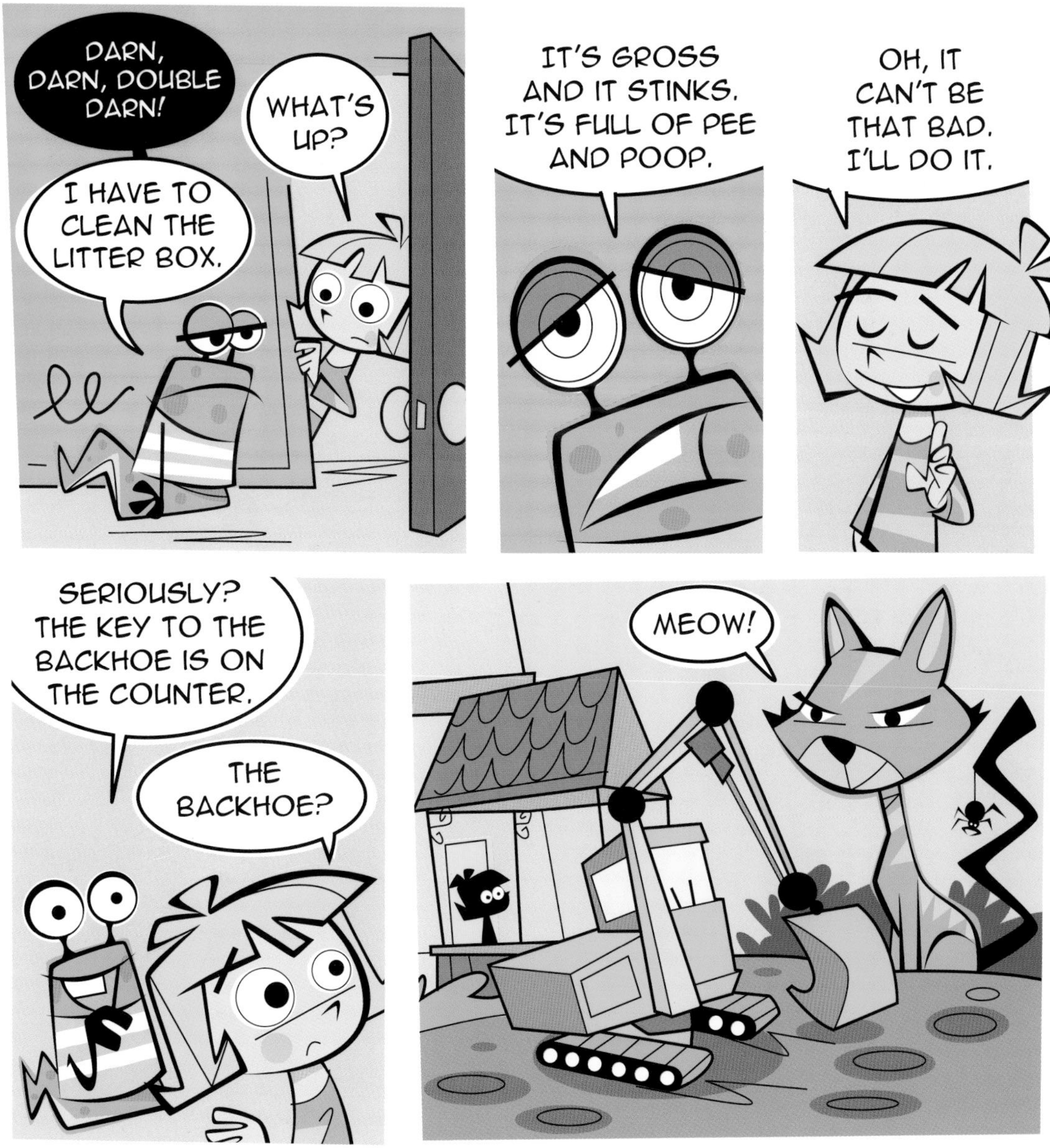
DARN, DARN, DOUBLE DARN!
WHAT'S UP?
I HAVE TO CLEAN THE LITTER BOX.
IT'S GROSS AND IT STINKS. IT'S FULL OF PEE AND POOP.
OH, IT CAN'T BE THAT BAD. I'LL DO IT.
SERIOUSLY? THE KEY TO THE BACKHOE IS ON THE COUNTER.
THE BACKHOE?
MEOW!

Success!

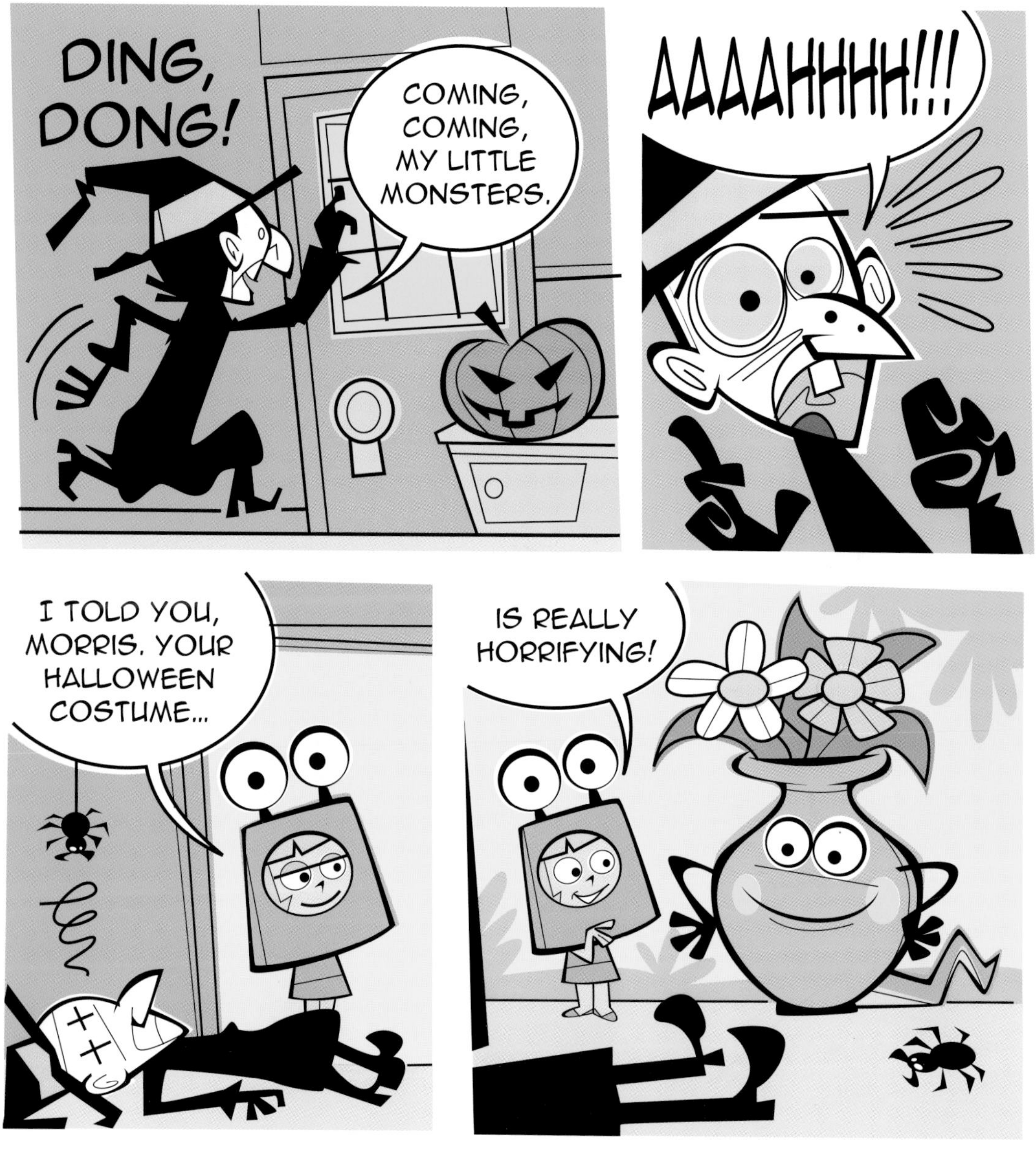
DING, DONG!
COMING, COMING, MY LITTLE MONSTERS.
AAAAHHHH!!!
I TOLD YOU, MORRIS. YOUR HALLOWEEN COSTUME...
IS REALLY HORRIFYING!

Baby Proof

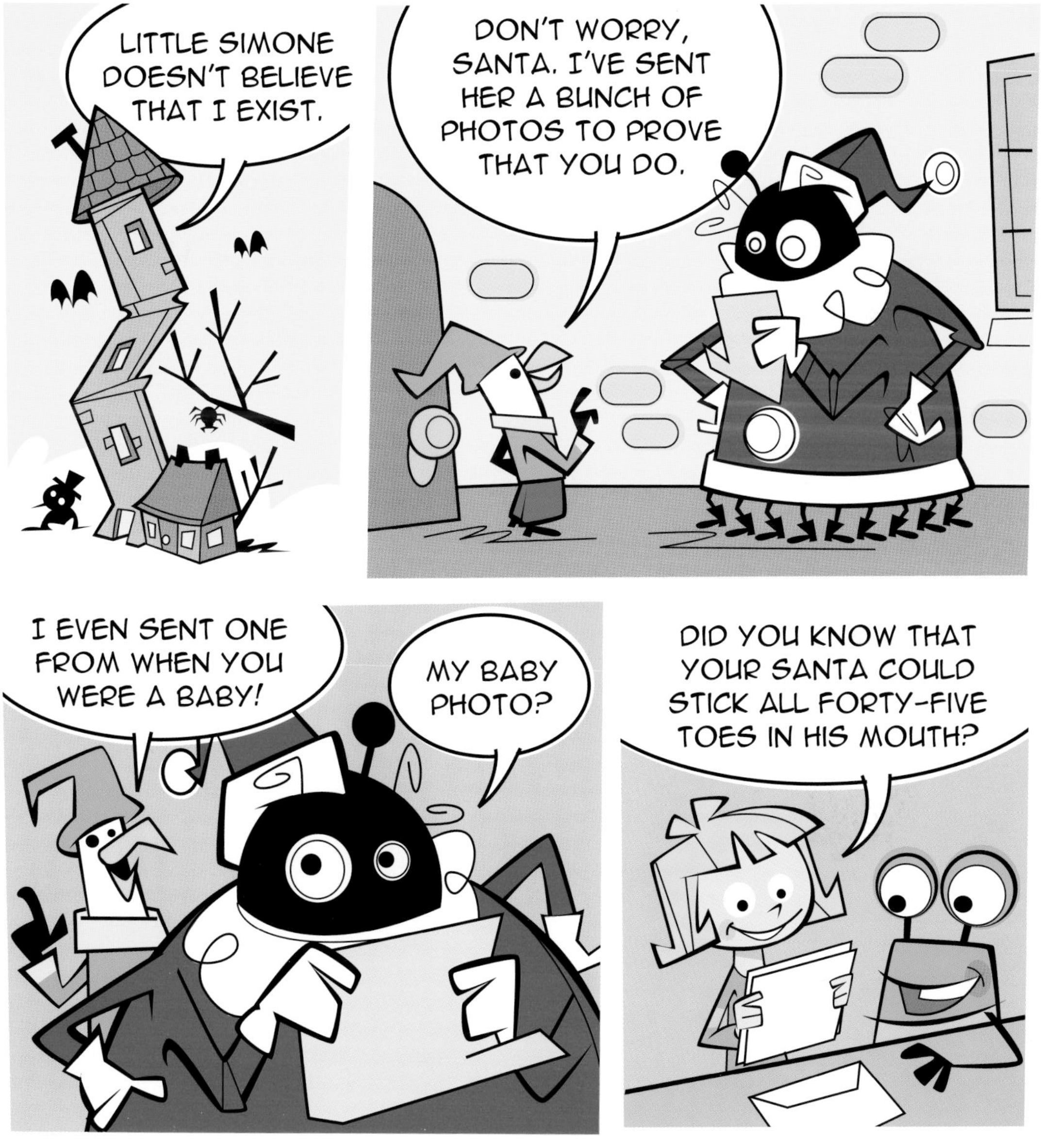
LITTLE SIMONE DOESN'T BELIEVE THAT I EXIST.
DON'T WORRY, SANTA. I'VE SENT HER A BUNCH OF PHOTOS TO PROVE THAT YOU DO.
I EVEN SENT ONE FROM WHEN YOU WERE A BABY!
MY BABY PHOTO?
DID YOU KNOW THAT YOUR SANTA COULD STICK ALL FORTY-FIVE TOES IN HIS MOUTH?

Finally, Some Peace!

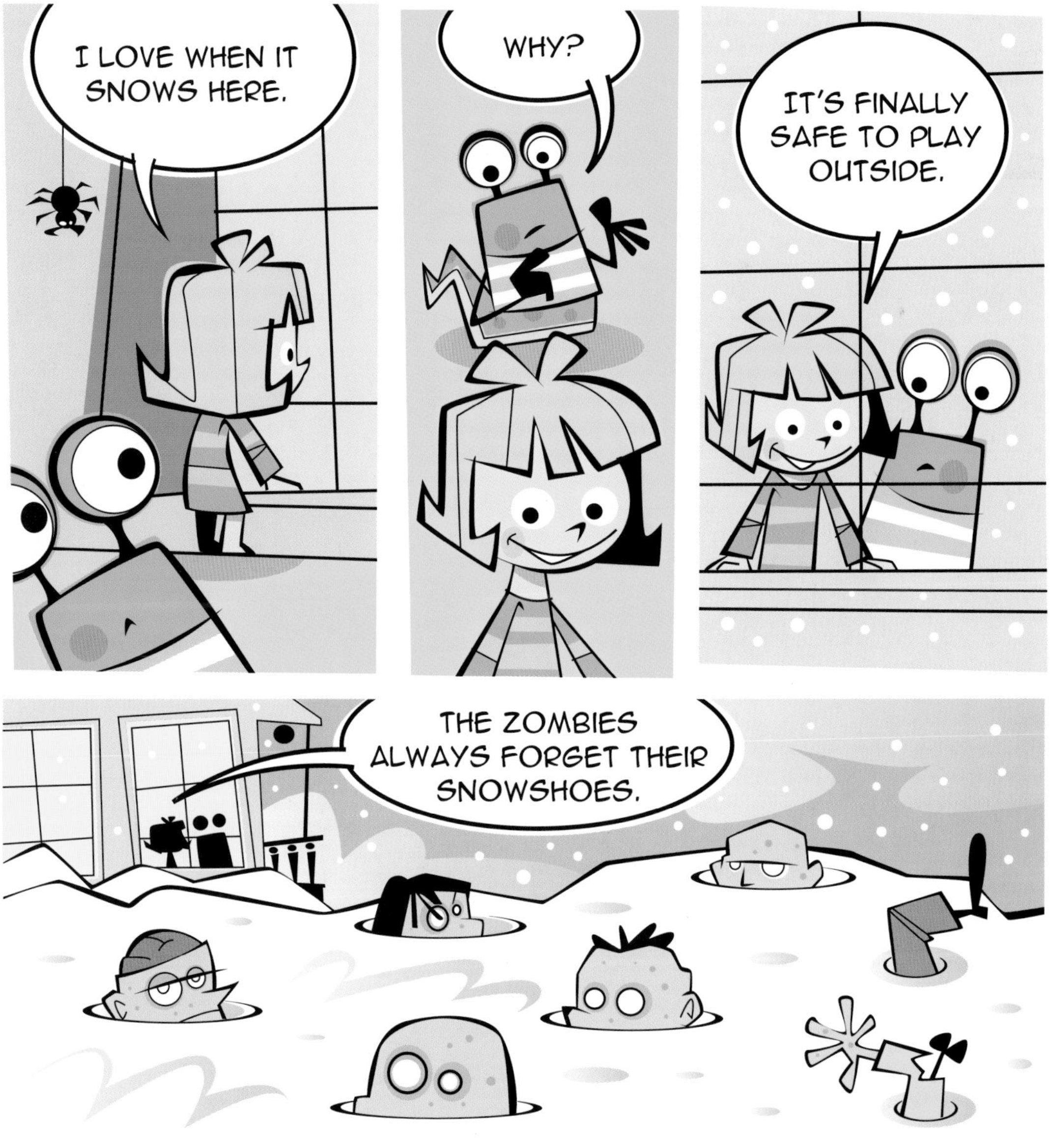
I LOVE WHEN IT SNOWS HERE.
WHY?
IT'S FINALLY SAFE TO PLAY OUTSIDE.
THE ZOMBIES ALWAYS FORGET THEIR SNOWSHOES.

Time-Out!

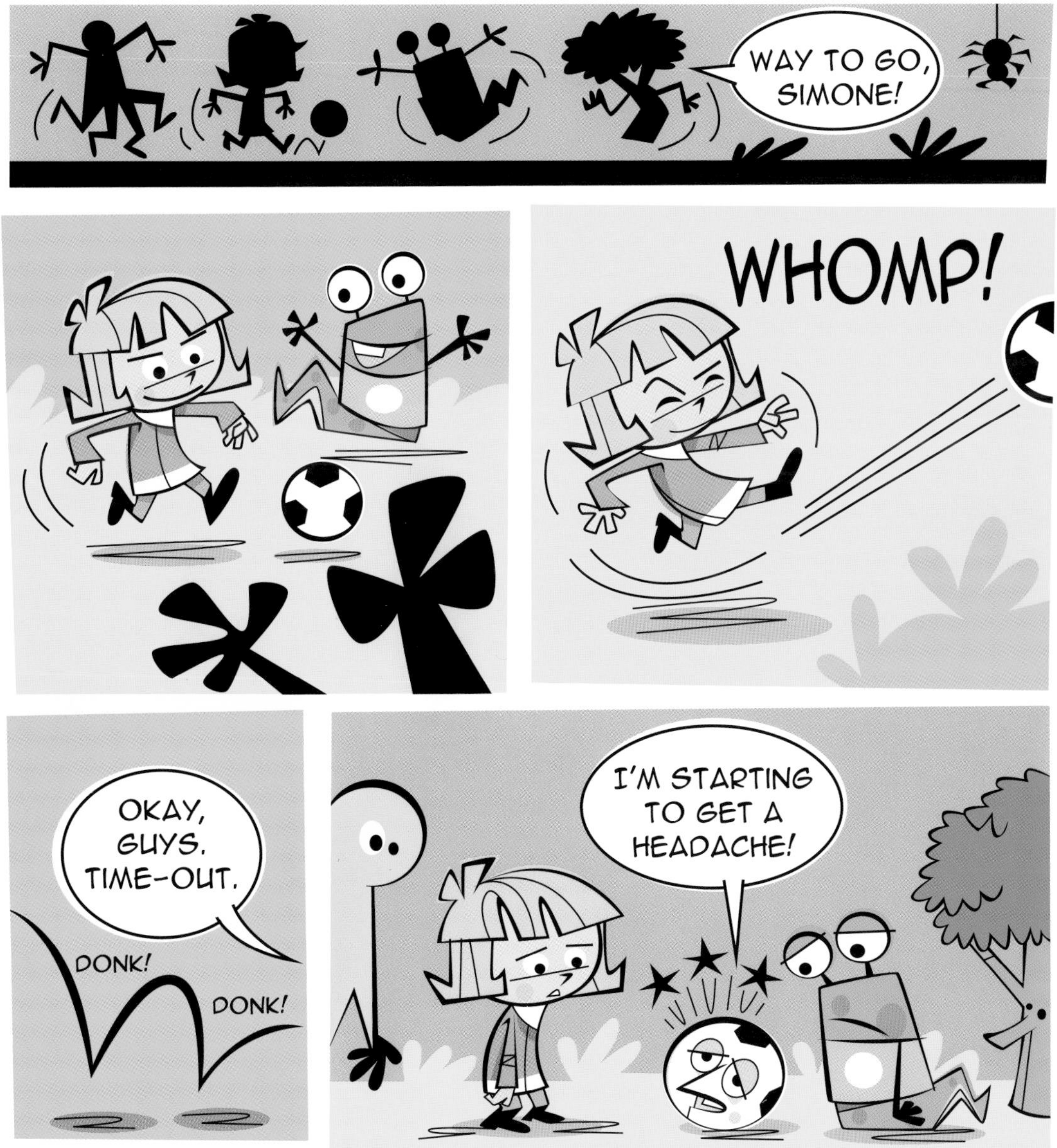
WAY TO GO, SIMONE!
WHOMP!
OKAY, GUYS. TIME-OUT.
DONK!
DONK!
I'M STARTING TO GET A HEADACHE!

Nightmare

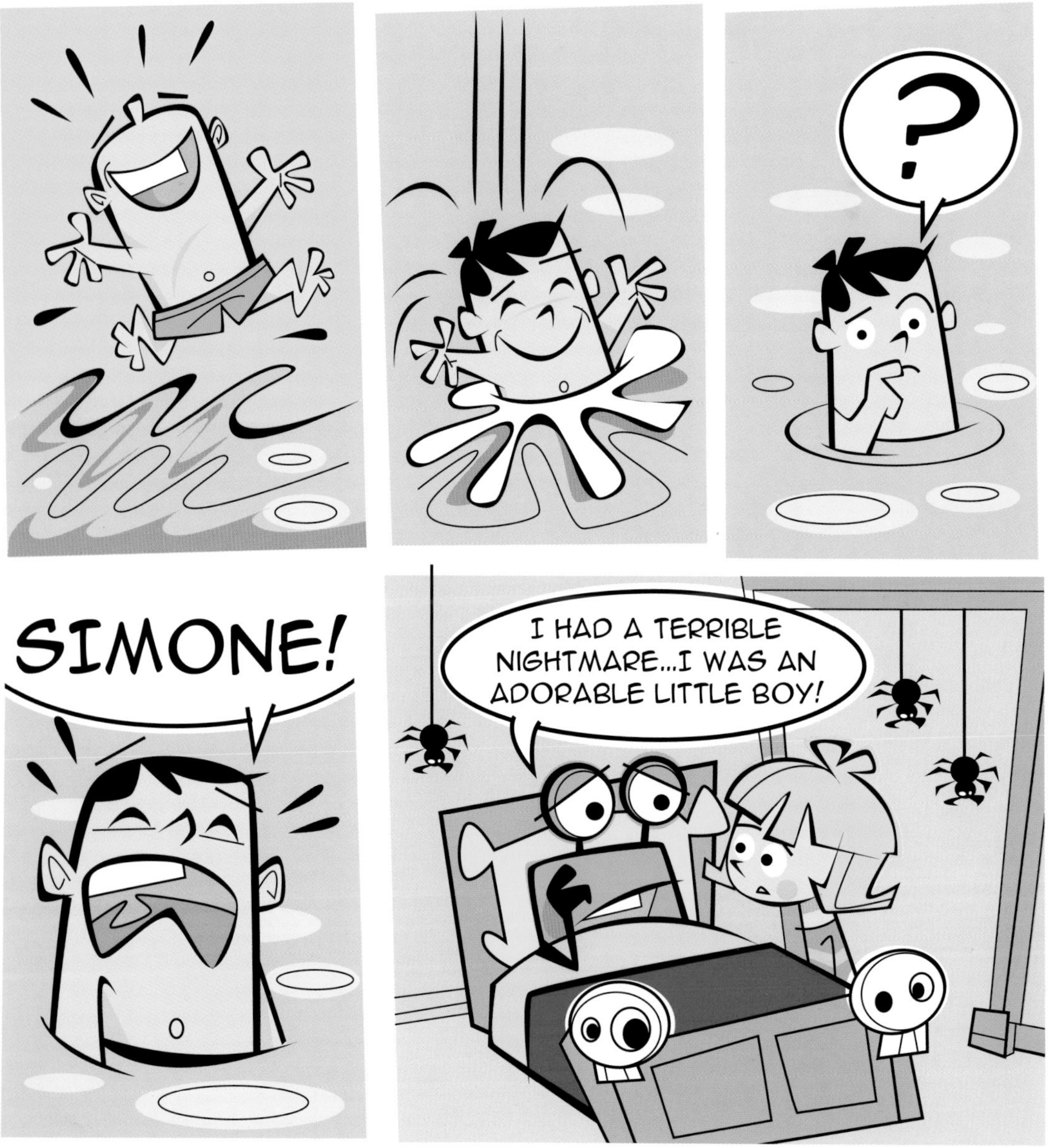
?
SIMONE!
I HAD A TERRIBLE NIGHTMARE...I WAS AN ADORABLE LITTLE BOY!